faith

A Harmless World Novel

The Wulf Family
Book One

melissa schroeder

harmless publishing

contents

also by
melissa schroeder

The Melissa Schroeder Instalove Collection

- Dominion Rockstar Romance
- Mafia Sisters
- Faking It
- Single Titles

The Camos and Cupcakes World

- Camos and Cupcakes
- The Fillmore Siblings
- Juniper Springs-coming soon

The Santini World

- The Santinis
- Semper Fi Marines
- The Fitzpatricks

The Harmless World

- The Harmless Series
- A Little Harmless Military Romance
- Task Force Hawaii

Check out the rest of Mel's books by:

- Interest
- Series
- Entire Backlist

about the author

From an early age, USA Today Best-selling author Melissa loved to read. When she discovered the romance genre, she started to listen to the voices in her head. After years of following her AF Major husband around, she is happy to be settled in Northern Virginia surrounded by horses, wineries, and many, many Wegmans.

Keep up with Mel, her releases, and her appearances by subscribing to her NEWSLETTER or join in the fun with her Harmless Addicts!

Check out all her other books, family trees and other info at her website!
If you would want contact Mel, email her at: melissa@ melissaschroeder.net

instagram.com/melschro
amazon.com/author/melissa_schroeder
facebook.com/MelissaSchroederfanpage
x.com/melschroeder
bookbub.com/authors/melissa-schroeder
goodreads.com/Melissa_Schroeder

meet the wulf siblings

They come from privilege and power, a stone's throw away from the British royal family. But these siblings know how to get dirty when it comes to life.

Faith

Jensen Wulf had no idea the one woman he could never live without in business was the woman he needed in his bed. He just has to convince the contrary woman he loves her.

Taboo

Julienne Wulf has always played the good girl, in her business and her personal life. Unfortunately, she's fallen for a totally inappropriate man who knows exactly how to make her be bad.

Trust

Jakob Wulf has always been in love with one woman. After a night he has yet to forget, she walks out of his life. Once she shows back up, he is determined to prove his love.

To Ruth Jean Bodnar
You introduced me to a world filled with Winnie the Pooh and
Peter Rabbit. You always supported my love of reading from
library trips to buying every Trixie Belden every published. I am
the writer I am today because you were the mother you were. I
miss you more each and every day.

hawaiian terms

Aloha - Hello, goodbye, love
Bra-Bro
Bruddah- brother, term of endearment
Haole-Newcomer to the islands
Hiwahiwa - precious
Howzit - How is it going?
Kama'āina-Local to the islands
Mahalo-Thank you
Malasadas- A Portuguese donut without a hole which started out as a tradition for Shrove (Fat) Tuesday. They are deep fried, dipped in sugar or cinnamon and sugar. In other words, it is a decadent treat every person must try when they go to Hawaii. If you do not try it, you fail. Do yourself a favor. Go to Leonard's and buy one. You are welcome.
Pupule - crazy
Slippahs - slippers, AKA sandals

prologue

Four years ago

J ensen Wulf let himself into his New York brownstone and sighed with relief. It had been a long three months since he'd been here, in what he had termed as his *sanctuary*. He'd left on his own accord, ready to make a fresh start and walk away from the heroin haze he'd lived in over the last four years.

The apartment smelled fresh. The vinegary scent of heroin no longer clung to the furniture. He assumed that his mother had made sure everything had been cleaned out before he returned. She was good like that. She kept things tidy, even as everything else was falling apart. The floors had been redone, there was a new coat of paint throughout... damn, he owed her.

He had disappointed her, more than a few times, but almost dying of an overdose was the worst. He would never forget the look of pain in her gaze. It was that look that had made him realize he wasn't just hurting himself.

There was mail stacked up on a credenza. His mother

had taken care of the bills, he knew that. But, he was sure there was other correspondence for him. He picked up the envelopes and stepped into the living room.

He didn't see her at first. She was sitting in the chair to the right of the fireplace, her phone in her hand as she read something on the screen.

"I thought you would never make it in here."

American, but there was a slight accent to her voice that he couldn't place. She was dressed in a striking red blouse, a short black skirt, hose, and fuck me heels. Her hair was dark brown and long from what he could tell. She had it up in a ponytail. A black coat was draped over the arm of the chair.

"Excuse me?"

She looked up at him. Ice blue eyes. Jesus, it didn't fit with the rest of the package.

"You spent a lot of time in the foyer."

He opened his mouth to explain why, then he remembered it was *his* fucking house.

"Who the hell are you?"

She smiled, but there was little humor behind it.

"Nicola McCann."

The name was familiar, but he was sure he had never met her.

"And you are sitting in my house for what reason?"

"Your mother hired me."

"For what?"

"I'm your sober companion. We're going to be best friends for the next three months."

chapter one

Hawaii, Present Day

Nicola stepped off the last stair from the private jet and cursed her life. Okay, she sounded like a bitch, even to herself…in her own head. She had flown from LA to Honolulu on a private jet, and she was cursing her life. Rich people problems, indeed.

She slipped on her sunglasses and ignored the bead of sweat that had already formed on her back and was now slowly rolling down her spine. She was not a woman made for tropical beaches or humidity. Before she was eighteen, she had spent most of her life in an ice rink. She longed for a day in the snow, drinking hot chocolate, and riding a sled.

"Move it along, Nic," Jensen said from behind her, irritation easy to hear in his voice.

He didn't like being here anymore than she did. Hawaii was gorgeous, but she had a feeling Jensen's irritation arose from the laidback style of Hawaii. He had a lot of time on his hands when he was here, and he knew that's when he made mistakes. *Mistakes*, that's what they called it since the one time he had gone on a bender three years ago. Idle hands and all of that.

She stepped aside and waited for him to take the lead. She followed behind him, not out of duty, but it was the easiest way to get things done. Nicola gave up duty a long time ago.

"Did you contact Micah Ross?" he asked.

"Yes. He knows you are on the island today."

One way to make sure he kept himself occupied was through the BDSM club, Rough 'n Ready. If he could find a sub or two to play with while on his business trip, Jensen would keep his nose and arm clean. She wasn't sure if that made her a pimp, but she was fairly certain it didn't. Jensen didn't have to pay for subs. They clamored for him. And lately, for some unknown reason, she'd started to get pissed about it.

"Good. I guess you can drop me off there on the way to the house."

She blinked. "What?"

He glanced back at her. "I want you to drop me off."

They'd just arrived on the island and it was the middle of the day. "Jensen, they're not open this early."

He blinked as if just realizing it was sunny out. "Oh."

"Let's go to the house, check in, you can clean up, change and then head out."

He didn't look happy about the situation, but he nodded and slid into the sedan.

She shook her head and walked around to the other side of the car. This was probably not going to be a good trip. Lately, a lot of their trips had been uncomfortable. There was something off about Jensen, and she didn't know what it was.

Her old sober companion instincts had reared their ugly

head, but Jensen was going to meetings. A lot of meetings, but he was going. In fact, he had insisted that he make sure the listed times they had from their last visit to the islands was correct.

She slipped into the backseat of the limo, and looked over her schedule.

"Remember, day after tomorrow, you are going to Maui for a meeting with the Johnson family."

He grunted, which meant he was at least listening to her. "Johnson? Doesn't sound very Hawaiian."

He'd already remarked on that—several times.

"No Hawaiian family can claim one hundred percent Hawaiian blood. At least not many."

"I thought these wankers were fighting us because we aren't Hawaiian?"

"They are, in a way. They are trying to preserve the beauty of Hawaii."

He shot her a dirty look. "You've been against this development from the beginning."

She nodded. "I think there is no reason for it and I agree with the locals."

He snorted and looked out the window.

"And what was that for?"

"It seems to me to be hypocritical."

"Why?"

"You make a living being my assistant. Therefore, you would stand to gain from the deal."

"First, I only get paid my salary."

"Which is insanely high."

She was getting sick of this argument. "And, if you sign a deal with the Johnson family, that doesn't make me any richer. Also, I can disagree with what you do and still work for you."

"Is that a fact?"'

She didn't like his tone. She called it his royal *we* voice. He always used it when he thought he was above everyone else. Dismissing him, she tried her best to concentrate on the work at hand. She had a billion emails to answer, but Nicola ignored them. Instead, she texted her best friend Serenity to tell her she had arrived.

On island.

About damned time. When will I see you?

As soon as his lord Wulf leaves for the club tonight.

Good. Mick said he will make your favorite shrimp.

One of these days, I will steal that big hunk of man from you.

Good luck, loser. You have to fight Adam and me for him.

Nicola smiled. Her friend had found her soulmates just a year earlier and Nicola was so happy for her. Still, she was a little envious. Both of them had forever wondered if they would find even one man to trust. Serenity found two.

"What?"

She glanced up at Jensen, who was watching her intently.

"What, what?"

"Why are you smiling?" he asked.

"Nothing. Just Serenity."

"Ah. So, you're going to go over *there* tonight." He sounded like he was accusing her.

"And? You don't need me. You're going to the club."

He mumbled something under his breath as he turned to look out the window.

"You're mumbling again."

"I said that you spend a lot of time with them."

It was her turn to blink.

"What do you mean by that?"

He turned back to her. "You just seem to spend a lot of time with that threesome."

"I get to see Serenity very seldom, so when we are here, I spend as much time as I can with her."

"And them."

"Excuse me?"

He rolled his eyes. "And them. Those men."

"You liked them before."

"That was different."

"Jensen, are you sure you haven't scored recently? Have you started using again?"

"That's not funny."

"What am I supposed to think? You're saying insane things."

He opened his mouth, then snapped it shut.

"Exactly. Serenity is in a committed relationship with two men. They are not swingers. But, I have been promised my favorite dish when I come to the islands."

"Shrimp truck shrimp."

"Yes," she said, a little surprised that he knew.

"What? I pay attention. Besides, you're out at Giovanni's constantly. And you got Freddy to learn the recipe just how you like it."

She smiled and then started going through her emails. She didn't want him to know exactly how stupid happy that made her.

"Dinner with the trio, then?"

"Yes. Serenity did ask if we were all going out while we were here."

"Sure."

But that meant nothing. Lately, Jensen had been acting oddly. More than odd. He had been avoiding her. And, since he had a past and was a recovering addict, she had worried. Still, it was the only sign, so she had reserved judgement.

She glanced at him once more. He was looking out the window again, ignoring her. It was hard to believe they were four years down the road. She had taken the job at the pleading of his mother. It was one she hadn't wanted, since Jensen had a reputation of being a bad boy. Being a blood relative of the Windsors did not help. People loved to do things for and to him. She had avoided working with those kinds of addicts. Still, it was hard to ignore a plea from a mother who loved her son so much. Little did she know, it would be the last work she did in the field.

"I take it you don't need me next week, do you?"

He shrugged. Good God, she was not in the mood for this. She could push him, but it would just make him react more like an ass. So, she followed his lead and looked out the window. The midday traffic wasn't heavy. Late October wasn't a big tourist time for Hawaii. The landscape flew past her as they drove down H-1. They'd bought a house on Portlock Rd. House? More like compound. She was just a girl who grew up in a small Colorado town in a two-bedroom home. The Wulf's would have no idea what that was like. *Ever*.

"You like these men?"

She turned her head. He wasn't looking at her, but had laid his head against the back of the seat and had his eyes closed. "What?"

"You like Adam and Mick?"

"I like that they make my friend happy. She's had enough bad times to last a lifetime. That the two of them see it as their mission in life to keep her happy make them gods in my opinion."

"Hmm."

Then, silence again. She knew this was a tactic he used in business. Jensen lulled people into thinking he was a bad boy without any brains. The proverbial rich boy who cared more about his money than people. They would be wrong. As much as she hated to admit it, there was a world class brain in that beautiful head of his, and he *did* care about people. Like the rest of the family, his English upbringing sometimes got in the way of showing it, but it was there.

"What does that mean?" she asked.

"Just that they are all members of Rough 'n Ready."

"And?"

"You seem to look down on me for being a member."

"I do not."

He opened an eye. "Really?"

His tone told her he didn't believe her.

"No. If you remember, I suggested that you look into BDSM as an outlet."

He sat up and opened both eyes. "So, why the judgement in your voice?"

"I'm not judging you. I worry about you. That's all."

The leather creaked as he moved closer. He was so close she could feel his body heat. The scent of his aftershave filled her senses and left her a little lightheaded. She had to fight off the shiver. "That's it?"

She nodded. "I've heard that the club is one of the best in the world. I have never, and will never, judge you for your need for Domination. I promise."

He stayed close a moment longer, then sighed. "Good. Because I would blame it all on you," he said, but this time his voice was lighter, less sarcastic. He leaned back again and she breathed a sigh of relief.

If he ever figured out she was also a member, he would never let her hear the end of it.

JENSEN WAS out of the car before it came to a complete stop. He needed space, away from Nic, away from it all. Mostly…her. God, he'd had to deal with the long flight over, and now this.

He made sure to keep all of his feelings buried beneath the surface. Nic would not be happy about them. Or how many times he'd awakened with a hard-on in the last two months after a hot dream of her. More than once he'd had to fight the urge to go to her. Now, they were in romantic Hawaii and she would insist on wearing those fucking little bikinis.

"Jensen?" He realized she'd walked past him to the front door. Marta, the housekeeper, had already opened it.

"Sorry. Jet lag."

She gave him a look that told him she didn't believe him, but she didn't push it. One of the bad things about having his former sober companion as his personal assistant—she just didn't put up with his shit.

At least there would be no thigh highs here. Granted, he had never gotten proof of what she was wearing, but he was a man who knew silk stockings when he saw them. He particularly liked the back seamed ones.

Jensen fought off a shudder. Even as he thanked the gods that he was avoiding short skirts and stockings, he knew she was going to be wearing short skirts to show off her tanned legs, and camisoles that bared even more of her skin.

"Come on. Get changed and go out to Rough 'n Ready. I'm not in the mood to deal with you anymore. Aloha, Marta. Howzit?"

He loved the way that no matter where they were, she could slip into the local language and slang. It was her way of showing respect. He knew it came from all her travels in her skating competition days, but it had appealed to him. It made him look smarter. There was the added thrill he got when she spoke another language. Italian was a particular favorite of his.

"Everything is good, Nicola."

"Great. We really don't need you tonight. I ate on the plane and I'm heading over to my friend's house later. Mr. Wulf is going out tonight."

"Of course," Marta said as she stepped back to let both of them come into the house.

They had never owned property on the islands before. It wasn't a place they had any interest in until a year or two ago. Because of the frequent trips, though, the family had decided to buy another house. This one had become a partic-ular favorite of his. It boasted an open floor plan with floor to ceiling windows that looked out on the Pacific. The light paint on the walls, along with amazing views, gave the house an airy feel.

"Everything looks wonderful," Nic said. "But then, that's what I've come to expect."

Marta beamed as she followed them down the hall. Nic always knew what to say to people to let them know she appreciated their work. It was one of the things he liked about her and also one of the reasons he'd hired her as his PA.

Today, it just made him cranky. Cranky and horny.

Bloody hell.

"I stocked the fridge to your specifications; plus, I found some fruit at the farmer's market I thought you would like."

"You are a goddess, Marta. What would I do without you?" Nic asked.

Again, the right thing.

"Thank you, Marta," he said. She smiled at him and hurried out to organize everything that had come in from the car.

"I would suggest an ice-cold shower."

"What?" he asked turning on Nicola. How did she know?

"I said, that maybe you should take an ice-cold shower. You need to cool off and calm down."

His phone rang before he could respond. His brother's ring so he clicked it on.

"Bloody hell, I just got here."

"I love you, too," Jakob said.

"What do you want?"

"I just thought I would check and make sure everything worked out and you're there alive."

"You probably already talked to Frank, so why is that a problem?"

His brother was responding when Nicola took the phone from him.

"Hello, Jakob. Don't try to irritate your brother. He's already irritated and then I'll have to deal with him."

She was silent for a moment or two. Jensen fought the need to grab the phone out of her hand. Lately, he'd been getting irritated how much she and Jakob talked on the phone. And in person. Every now and then, they sat next to each other at meals. That was getting really annoying.

He rolled his eyes. Good lord. He was starting to sound like a teenager with a crush on his teacher. He was actually jealous of his brother for no other reason than he was talking to Nic. There was no good reason for the two of them to talk.

Jakob had a very small role at the company since he spent most of his time acting.

"I see. Well, if the Johnsons don't want to meet with us—"

Silence again as his brother talked.

"Oh, okay. I got it. They want to have a meeting next week on Maui. I'll get everything set up. Just send me the particulars. Do you want to talk to Jensen again?"

His brother responded, which brought out a bubble of laughter from Nicola. "Okay."

She clicked off his phone and handed it back to him. Then she started to walk away. He grabbed hold of her arm, which was a mistake. Touching her was always a mistake.

She glanced down at his hand, then back up to his face. "Yes?"

"Do you want to tell me what that was all about?"

"Meeting next week on Maui. Seems the Johnsons are going to try and play hardball. You can let go of me now."

He didn't realize until that moment that his hands were still on her.

"Sorry." He waited one more second than was necessary and then released her arm.

"No worries. They want us on Maui next week. A meeting of the minds."

Dammit. He understood it wasn't easy to give up family land, but Wulf Industries wasn't going to do anything with it. Well, anything else than the family had been doing. The pristine land was prime vacation land, and they had a hotel on it. Wulf Industries wanted to redo the entire resort, update it, and bring in more jobs for the locals. Still, the Johnsons had been dragging their feet for months after they had already agreed to negotiate a price with them. They were the only bidder who had been willing to keep the resort island friendly.

"So, we're going over there next week?"

She shrugged as she started to walk away. "It would only be for overnight, so I guess we both don't need to go."

He breathed a sigh of relief. While he had enjoyed having her as a traveling companion in the past, his new attraction to her was getting out of hand. Being at a resort overnight... well, he did not want to test himself. Not right now.

"What will you do?"

"I might just lay out by the pool with Serenity and be a lazy tourist for a few days."

He blinked at the anticipation he heard in her voice. "That doesn't sound like you at all."

She stopped walking and turned around to face him. "What do you mean by that?"

Now what did he do? She was staring at him with those ice blue eyes of hers, and she expected an answer from him. And in that one instant, he couldn't think. Every bloody thought in his brain dissolved into visions of leaning forward and brushing his mouth over hers. She would be sweet, so sweet, with just the right amount of spice.

"I'm waiting," she said in the tone that told him she wasn't happy with him.

"Just that you never seem to settle down. I always thought taking a break for you was when you made lists."

She snorted. "Do you remember what I did for my last vacation?"

"I know you went to Arizona with Serenity."

She rolled her eyes. "I gave you the itinerary. You should have known where we were every day."

"Oh, yeah." He had ignored it. Mainly because he spent the entire week in a panic without her. Well, mildly panicked. He wasn't accustomed to spending so much of his time alone.

"We went to Mii Amo."

"You went to another resort other than ours?" he asked, irritated.

"Yes. Everyone knows my name at the three resorts we have in the US. They don't give me a moment's rest or let me act like a tourist, so I went somewhere else. And, do you know what I did the entire time I was there?"

He could not speak, so he shook his head.

"I rested. I gorged myself on some amazing food, and I had so many body treatments I can't even remember them all. Massages, body wraps, reiki…you name it and it was probably done to my body."

She closed her eyes and hummed. Good lord, she was trying to kill him. Just thinking about her naked on a table, slathered with oils and lotions, had what little blood left in his brain traveling down to his cock. Fuck.

When she opened her eyes, she was smiling. "And I loved it. It was fantastic. In fact, we are planning another one later this year and I cannot wait. So, for your information, I do know how to relax."

When he said nothing, she frowned.

"Are you okay, Jensen?"

He nodded, but he still didn't talk.

"You should at least jump in the shower to wash the grime off you. You're pretty, but I'm sure whatever sub you find tonight doesn't want a stinky Dom."

He nodded again.

"I'm going to take one myself before heading over to Serenity's. If I don't see you before you leave, have fun, but play safe."

And with that, she trotted up the stairs as if she hadn't just given him a vivid picture of herself as she lay naked.

"Sir?" Marta said when she walked back into the foyer.

He shook himself out of his stupor and gave their house-keeper a smile. "No worries. Just a little jetlag. A shower will fix all that."

But even as he made his way to his second-floor bedroom, he knew he was lying. The only way the shower would work was if it were ice cold. He really hated when Nic was right.

chapter two

J ensen stepped out of the car and smiled at John. "Thanks. I'll text you when I'm ready to go."

"Sure thing, sir."

Jensen was smiling when he flashed his card to the doorman and then walked into Rough 'n Ready. Years ago, Nicola had suggested that maybe he needed to explore his need for control. He had thought she meant going to a therapist, but instead, she sent him to a Dominatrix who taught him exactly what he needed in the bedroom. His need to control his environment, and failing at that, had sent him running to drugs. Now, he had this.

He stood at the top of the stairs and took in the crowd. It was Saturday night, so the place was packed. Of course, it was busy on the weeknights also, but Saturdays were probably their best nights. Jensen enjoyed Rough 'n Ready. It was well-run and always packed with a good group of people. The regulars were great, but being in a vacation spot like Honolulu, he could always count on someone new to meet. The black and red interior was common in many clubs, but the layout was different. Ross and his partner Evan Chambers understood that just because you were at the club, you didn't always want to play. Being among people who understood who you were, that was a comfort.

The private rooms were filled with the best equipment, and the open area included a bar—only for those not playing for the night—and ample seating. The best part about it was what he called the stadium. There was an opening in the floor that served as a demonstration area. While many people would assume that a BDSM club in Hawaii would be a little more than a tourist attraction, Rough 'n Ready was so much more than that. They brought in people from all over the world for classes and demonstrations; and boasted every well-known Dom and Domme on the islands as members and/or teachers.

He was only about halfway across the floor when he spotted Micah Ross, one of the two owners of Rough 'n Ready. Jensen changed his direction, so he could chat up the Native American Dom. Ross would have the best idea on who was willing and able to take up for some fun for a night.

When people thought of the quintessential Native American, Micah Ross could be the poster boy. Tall, stoic, with long, black, straight hair, he dominated any room he was in. Even as crowded as the club was, there was no doubt he drew most eyes when he walked through the gathering. It had nothing to do with him being the owner of the club, and everything to do with the man.

"Hey, Wulf," he said with a smile and handshake. "How's tricks?"

"Ross. Seems the club is hopping tonight."

"As usual, thankfully."

"It shouldn't be a surprise to you."

His lips twitched. "I never take anything for granted."

"Indeed. I know better than most."

"I talked to the very attractive Ms. McCann. She didn't say how long you'll be here."

He shrugged. "At least a couple of weeks. Maybe a month"

"Good. We have some great classes and demonstrations coming up."

"Indeed. Think I need to learn something, Ross?"

"A refresher course never hurts."

"True."

"More than a few willing subs here tonight. Lord knows they would clamor at a chance with the Bad Boy Billionaire."

He winced. "Oh, God, not you too."

"I thought you liked the name."

He had at one time. It was heady being named by the press. He'd been twenty-two at the time and full of idiotic ideas.

"I would rather just be called Jensen or Sir."

Ross' lips twitched again. "I can understand that. How long have you been on the island?"

He didn't like the idea that Ross seemed to be so familiar with Nic. "Just a few hours ago. Tell me, Ross, how well do you know Nic?"

The other man's eyebrows rose. "What are you asking?"

He didn't want to say it because saying it would make him look like an ass. Ross was in love with his wife and never played outside the bounds of marriage. Why would he think Ross was messing around with Nic? Besides, Jensen had no say in what Nic did in her personal life.

Micah was still watching him, and that was a dangerous thing. Jensen shrugged, then pretended interest in a group of women who walked by.

"Nothing really. Just that you called her very attractive. I thought you hadn't met in person."

"Hmm, no. Just in pictures with you, and of course in her days on the ice. Other than that, I've only talked to her on the phone."

Jensen didn't respond. It was a stupid reaction that had been plaguing him in recent months. Jealousy. Bloody hell, he wasn't involved with her. He had no right to her. He didn't get jealous of his lovers. He didn't like attachments, and usually stayed away from entanglements.

"Don't you think she's hot?" Ross asked.

He shrugged, trying to pretend disinterest. "Sure. But she's not my type."

"And what type would that be? She's stunning."

She was. It was what had been keeping him up at night. "Yes, but can you see her being a sub? You've dealt with her on the phone."

Micah gave him a side eye glance. "I don't know her *that* well."

"Now, what the bloody hell does that mean?" Jensen asked with little heat.

"I've been in this business for a few years. I was a bounty hunter back in the day, so I know a little bit about human nature. People rarely show their true selves to the world."

"I know that. It took my family three years to know I was a heroin addict."

"You just proved my point."

Jensen chuckled. "Either way, I'm off to find someone to play with tonight."

"Have fun, but play safe."

The phrase caught his attention. It was the exact same thing that Nicola said.

"What did you say?"

"I said have fun."

"But play safe. Where did you hear that?"

He shrugged. "I've said it for years."

"Ah, okay. See you later, Ross."

The club owner nodded but said nothing else. Jensen headed off in the direction of Latochia, a rather frisky sub he'd played with last time he'd been at Rough 'n Ready. It was time to get himself back on track.

NICOLA PARKED her rental car just as her phone started to ring. She smiled thinking it would be Serenity calling to complain at her tardiness, but it was Jeffery Smyth, a skater she knew from her competition days.

"Hey, you, what are you doing calling me so late?"

"Because I talked to your mother earlier today, and she told me that you are in Hawaii, which Ben and I are too."

Most people would find it odd that he had a relationship with her mother, but skaters could be a very cloistered bunch. Long hours of training left them with little time for a social life outside of the rink. When his own parents turned away from him when he came out ten years earlier, her mother had welcomed him with open arms.

"Here? In Hawaii? On Oahu?"

"Yes. Yes, and no. We are on Maui, but when I heard you were going to be here, I was hoping you would be up for a lunch. Ben and I have some business early next week."

Out of all of her friends from those days, Jeffery was the only one who had not blamed her for walking away or for Oliver's death. Since leaving the business, he had become very successful at selling his brand, including a crazy reality show.

"This isn't going to be on the show?"

"Darling, the show ended about two years ago. You really *are* out of touch. It's just that it's been longer since we've seen you and we want to see you."

"Okay. I am free a lot next week because Jensen is actually going over to your island for a visit. Text me the particulars, and we can set something up."

"Sounds great. Going out?"

"I am out."

"Oh, and what kind of beautiful men are there? Describe them for me."

She chuckled. "The only two I'm going to see are completely committed to my friend Serenity and each other. They wouldn't have eyes for you."

"You need a life, Nicola."

"You need to butt out, Jeffy."

He gasped. "You promised never to use that name."

She laughed again. "I love you. Text me."

"Love you, too."

She was just stepping out of the car when Serenity came running out of the house and practically slammed into her. The attack hug took Nicola by surprise, causing her to stumble back into the car. Serenity Jones was small, but she was mighty.

She hugged her friend back as fiercely as Serenity hugged her. She was the only person in the world that Nicola completely trusted, and vice versa. Well, until Serenity had found Adam and Mick.

"Okay, that's enough," Nicola said with a laugh, as she untangled herself from Serenity.

Just a shade over five-foot-four, Serenity looked like the

girl next door. Big brown eyes, blonde locks, along with that dimpled smile, she fooled everyone. Nicola knew there was a world class and quite devious mind that operated in her cute head. The darkness that she had seen in her all those years ago when they'd first met was no longer there. Now, only joy sparkled in her eyes. Her whole body practically glowed with it.

"God, you look happy."

"That's because I am," she said.

She glanced back at the house and blinked. For once, the guys weren't standing there.

"Where are the guys?"

"They're out back on the lanai drinking beers. Rice is cooked, and salad is made. Mick said he would wait for our special guest."

"Oh, how fancy. I'm a special guest."

She looped Nicola's arm with hers. "So, how was the trip?"

"Long and boring. Jensen was a pain, but that is nothing new."

"One of these days, you are just going to drop that man, and he isn't going to know how to function."

She shrugged. "Truth is, he has barely spent any time in my presence. I think he might be getting ready to fire me."

"Really? That's odd."

"You just can't think of anyone wanting to fire me, but believe me, it happens."

She smiled. "No, just something the guys said. But, before we go in there and talk to them, I have something to tell you."

"Okay."

"We're pregnant."

For a long second, Nicola's mind blanked. Then, delight

spilled through her. "Oh, I am so happy for you, girl." She pulled her back into her arms for a hug. "You are going to be the best mom."

"I am, and well, I have double the help, so it will be easy."

Nicola shook her head as she pulled back. "I've never seen you so happy or confident. It is beautiful."

"Oh, no," Serenity said. Tears welled up in her eyes.

"What did I say?"

"Nothing, just you made me even happier."

The screen door opened to reveal Adam. He was the epitome of what a blond surfer would look like, with a hint of danger. He was in a tank top and board shorts.

"She's crying again," he yelled back to Mick. He smiled at Nicola and kissed her on the cheek. "She cries all the time these days."

"How long have you known?" Nicola asked.

"Three days," Serenity said as she sniffled.

"Three days and you just told me?"

"I wanted to tell you in person!"

Nicola sighed as Mick appeared in the doorway. Dark to Adam's light, he had black hair and chocolate eyes.

"Has she stopped?" he asked with a grin, and another kiss on the cheek for Nicola.

She looked at her friend. "Sort of."

"She's been driving us crazy about telling you. Every day she has given us an hour and a minute update of your arrival," he said.

She chuckled. "Well, I'm happy for all of you. And I hear that I get shrimp truck shrimp tonight."

"That you do," Mick said as he slung his arm over her shoulders. "I made it extra spicy since I know what you like."

He held the door open for her and waited as Serenity followed her in.

"I was just on the phone with Jeffrey."

"Jeffrey Smyth?" Serenity asked.

"Yeah. He and Ben are here on the islands."

"Wait, you know those two?" Adam asked.

She nodded. "Jeffrey and I came up at the same time in ice skating."

"Are they filming here?" Serenity asked.

"No. Apparently their show went off the air two years ago." Serenity shrugged. She'd spent her childhood in front of the TV, so she avoided it now. "They're flying over from Maui to see me. Apparently, they were trying to hunt me down and got hold of Mom. Now I have no way to avoid lunch."

"Oh, stop it. You love those two."

She sighed. "Yeah, but I have a bad feeling about this. Like they are in search of something."

"I take it Jensen is on his way to Rough 'n Ready?" Mick asked.

"Yep. Maybe he can find himself a sub to work his irritation out on."

"What do you mean by that?" Adam asked as he set a glass of her favorite red blend in front of her.

She looked at Serenity. "Seriously, now I might have to fight you for both of them."

"You are avoiding the question," Adam said with a smile.

"I mean that he has been cranky. We flew from London to New York. We stayed for two days, then on to LA for one. Now here. He hasn't had time to let loose; going to the club and finding a willing sub usually works for him."

He studied her for a long moment.

"What does that look mean?" she asked.

He shrugged. "I think his irritation might be closer to home."

"Now what the bloody hell does that mean?"

He opened his mouth to respond, but Serenity stepped in. "Did you want to give me some ideas on a nursery?"

She dragged Nicola down the hallway to the opposite end of the house.

"What are you doing, Serenity?"

"Avoiding a discussion you don't want to have."

As they stepped into the half empty room, Nicola shook her head. "I have no idea what you're talking about."

"And let's leave it at that," Serenity said. "So, the guys are going to add another room, and move this stuff there. Or, do you think we should have the baby room over by us?"

"You aren't as smooth at deflecting as you think you are."

She smiled. "Yes, but you love me, so you will let me get away with it."

Nicola tried to look stern, but she broke down. "You suck."

"No comment."

Nicola chuckled. "I still want to know what he was talking about."

"You won't like it."

"That's what I do. I deal with the parts of life that people don't like. And, you also know that if you don't tell me, I will get it out of Adam. Those two are so easy to squeeze information from."

Serenity rolled her eyes. "That's why I wouldn't let them talk to you. They want to tell everyone I'm pregnant."

"They don't care who the father is, genetically I mean?"

"Nope. They're excited, that's it. They say it will be both of theirs."

"Well, they are good at sharing," she said.

Serenity stared at her for a second then snorted. "Yeah. They are good at that."

"So..."

"Okay, but don't bother me about it later. Deal with Adam."

"Scout's honor."

"You were never in the scouts any more than I was."

"Stop stalling, Jones."

"Okay. It wasn't that big, but Adam thinks that Jensen has a thing for you."

She frowned. "Really? I think he would rather I just didn't exist lately. He's been very difficult."

"See. I think he's crazy."

"What made him think that?"

"When you were dealing with that tabloid reporter last year, he said Jensen sounded in awe."

She rolled her eyes. "That all has to do with what I can do for him."

"*Exactly.*"

"He was weird about me coming over here tonight."

"What?"

"He was questioning me about Adam and Mick, like we were going to have an orgy."

Her eyes widened. "Really?"

"Yeah. I think it was because I made plans without him. I think he sees Adam and Mick as his friends or something. Like if they spend time with me, then they are cheating on him."

"Weird."

"Dinner's ready," Mick called out.

"You remember I told you I'm stealing him, right?"

"Just try, woman," Serenity said, slipping her arm around Nicola's. "And let's eat. Mama needs some food."

SEVERAL HOURS LATER, Nicola had just slipped into her rental when her phone buzzed. She was going to ignore it until she realized it was from Rough 'n Ready.

"Hello."

"Nicola, this is Micah."

"Hey, Micah. Is there a problem?"

"No. Not really. I was wondering if you think Wulf knows you're a member here."

"No. There's no way. Why?"

"He was acting weird tonight."

"How?"

"Just that he seemed preoccupied, and he didn't end up with a sub."

"What?"

"He's still here and has spent time with several women, but he hasn't taken anyone to a private room."

"Oh, that doesn't mean anything. Jensen can be picky."

"Okay. Just wanted to make sure you knew I didn't tell him anything."

"Micah, I know better than anyone you know how to keep a secret."

"Well, from everyone but Dee."

"Your wife knows you were my first Dom?"

"Yes."

"Okay."

He chuckled. "My wife is a different kind of woman. If anything, she wants to ask *you* questions."

Nicola chuckled. "I always said it would take a very special woman to tame Micah Ross, so I'm not surprised.

Call if there are any issues. I'm about to head back to the house right now."

"Will do, night."

"Night."

She hung up and started the car, waving her hand out the window to signal to Serenity that she was leaving. She pulled out onto the street, then waited at the light at Kam Highway. It was late, past eleven, and she was exhausted. Thankfully, it was cool enough to have the windows down in the car. Fresh air would keep her awake.

As she drove down Kam Highway, she marveled at the beauty. Even in the dark, it was easy to see why Hawaiians loved their home. It was amazing during the day, but the air at night was so sweet. It almost made her want to live here all the time, but she was a woman made for snow.

She'd just passed the lighthouse when she saw a car speeding up behind her. She didn't like this road that much to begin with, but she really hated when people drove too fast on it. Ignoring the person, she continued to drive. Then, they flashed their brights. It figured. She was about to hit the most twisty/turny part of the road. The driver slowed down, but as her heartbeat evened out, he sped up again, getting closer to her. Tightening her hands on the steering wheel, she paid no attention to the way her stomach twisted into a knot.

They continued on like that, the bastard slowing down then speeding up closer to her. About the time she was ready to scream, he turned off onto the road that headed to Koko Head State Park.

She was rattled, but she made it back to the house in one piece. When she walked inside, her legs were shaking. After kicking off her sandals, she forced herself to walk up the stairs and to her bedroom. Liquor had never been Jensen's thing, but she also didn't believe in tempting the addict. She kept a bottle of whiskey in her room.

She found it, grabbed one of the glasses, and poured two fingers of the liquid. She downed it in one long swallow. She poured herself another glass, but this time she sipped. With uneasy legs, she walked out onto her balcony. She was kind of a ninny. The fact that some asshole decided to play games shouldn't scare her so much. Still, it reminded her of her skating days and the obsessive fans she and Oliver had dealt with. They obsessed over their relationship, the ups and downs. Add in the fact that they were the ranked number one skating couple in the world, it made for a lot of crazed fans.

Sitting in one of the two chairs on the lanai, she closed her eyes. That was a lifetime ago with a girl who still believed in fairytales and happily ever after. When she opened her eyes, she was steadier. That girl might be gone, but she was pretty damned satisfied with the woman she had become.

chapter three

J ensen woke the next morning, his head pounding and his cock stiff. He'd barely slept. Every time he fell asleep, Nicola had been there in his dreams—her enticing body and seductive voice keeping him awake for hours. He glanced down at his erection and grimaced. What the fuck was wrong with him? Last night should have been easy. Just some fun time in a room, but every woman had left him cold.

Now, he wished he had that problem. There was no denying the tented sheet or the raging hard-on that acted as it's pole. So, instead of finding a willing woman, he had spent the night dreaming of Nic. His fantasies were getting out of hand. Hell, it had been so vivid, he was sure he could smell her scent on his sheets. He licked his lips. Fuck. He didn't need reality when he could still taste her from his dreams.

Fucking bloody, *bloody* hell.

The woman was driving him mental. He had never been this obsessed with anything in his life. Scratch that. Heroin.

That had been the one other instance that he hadn't been able to deal with his fixation.

What the fuck was he supposed to do about a woman who he couldn't have? *Ever*. Usually, he didn't become enamored. He had always believed he didn't have the gene that people talked about. Those people who fell in love, loved being in love, wanted to be in love. No, he was different. He had a friend liken it to a drug addiction. Jensen had already had that in his life. No. He wanted nothing to do with it. Or her.

There was that other side of it too. She worked for him. He would not disrespect her that way. He didn't want to give her up because she made life as a Wulf livable. And not just for him. She managed all of them so well, including his mother. That right there was more than any of them had hoped. He had to deal with her and he kind of liked having her around. He rolled his eyes and swung his legs over the side of his bed. He was a bloody mess.

He glanced toward the door, but knew he needed to do something about the hard-on before even attempting to get dressed and going down for breakfast. With a sigh, he pushed himself up and off the bed. He padded barefoot into the bathroom. The cool tile felt good beneath is feet. He still wasn't sure if it had been a good idea to buy the house, but he did like it. His brother had said it would be best to have a home base, and his sister had said she could use it for vacation. Neither of those two would probably spend much time there. The light, airy feeling usually left him feeling calm.

He turned on the water and stepped into the shower. He bit back a scream. It felt like ice pelting his flesh. Damn. This was worse than he had expected. Still, it was what he needed.

As he stood there, letting the water slide down over his

body and icicles form in his blood, it didn't do anything for his erection. He glanced down. The one-eye bastard stood at attention, soaked with cold water.

"Fuck."

He wrapped his hand around his cock and started to stroke it. He was painfully aroused, beyond just that morning erection. Each day seemed to get worse, but this morning the situation had gotten ten times worse than yesterday. The fact that he could still function enough to stand erect amazed him. No matter how he stroked himself, he didn't gain any relief. None. At this point, he was sure if he took an ice bath, it wouldn't subside.

Grimacing, he realized what he needed. Or rather who. His eyes slid closed and she immediately appeared there. Her hair was down, spilled over her shoulders like silk. Water slid down her breasts, dripping from her nipples. Jensen could almost hear that little sigh she had. She released it in pleasure, usually over some kind of chocolate treat, but every time she did, his cock stood at attention begging for her caress. That sound had haunted his dreams more than once. Now, he used the memory of it to aid his release. Faster and faster, he stroked his hand up and down his shaft. Pressure built as he imagined her there in the shower, kissing her way down his stomach to his cock. Her hand, her mouth on him. The image of those full lips wrapped around his dick as she looked up at him with her ice blue eyes pushed him over the edge. He came, groaning with relief as he allowed pleasure to wash over him.

Long moments later, he leaned against the wall as he let the water clean the cum off his body.

He had no problem with masturbation, and as an adult, he had no issues with guilt. Still, he felt...unfulfilled? No, he had come, but he wasn't truly satisfied. No. This was something else, entirely. It was as if the fantasy was no longer doing it for him. That his obsession with Nic was now leaning into unhealthy territory.

NICOLA SLIPPED OFF her sunglasses and looked out over the pool to the Pacific Ocean. She was an adult, in her thirties, but every time she called her mother, she felt as if she were thirteen years old and getting caught breaking curfew.

"Are you going to at least take some time off, Nicola?" her mother asked.

Nicola sighed. "Yes, Mama."

"You work too hard."

What she meant was Nicola had not given her any grandchildren. Nadia McCann was ready for grandchildren, and she didn't mind telling Nicola every chance she got. She still hadn't told her mother about Serenity's pregnancy. That would probably end badly for Nicola. Her mother would start discussing how much younger Serenity was than Nic.

"But will you have time to relax?"

"Yes. In fact, Jensen is going to Maui next week. I'm staying here and I plan on poolside relaxation and probably a massage or two."

"Good. You know working like you do could lead to other issues."

She didn't respond. Her mother was being a little pushier than usual. And that was saying something. Her mother emailed every crackpot report about fertility she found.

"Nicola."

"Do you have something bad to tell me? Are you and Dad doing okay?"

She noticed a movement out of the corner of her eye. It was Jensen walking across the lanai toward her. He had a massive cup of coffee in his hand. He was dressed down for the islands, or as dressed down as a Wulf would get in public. His tropical shirt was subdued in colors, but it had flecks of green within the design. His khaki pants were expertly tailored—no Wulf wore off the rack. He looked like a damned model. And, he looked...well, yummy. Dammit. Not yummy. No. He looked good. Good. And delicious. She wanted to take a big bite out of that perfect ass of his.

Dammit.

"Nicola, are you listening to me?"

"What? Sorry, *Ma*ma."

"I said your father wants to go to a couples-only retreat."

She blinked. The tone her mother used struck her as odd.

"I heard they are nice."

"Nicola. I know you do other things in your sex life that I do not."

Damn, she sometimes regretted telling her mother so much about her life. Too much maybe, but because of her childhood, her mother had been her best friend.

"I have no idea what you are talking about. Why are you opposed to couple's retreats?"

Jensen had walked out to look out over the ocean, but he turned and looked back over his shoulder. She shrugged.

"I am not into that."

"Into what?"

"Swinging."

She pulled the phone out from her ear and looked at it, then returned it to her ear. "Excuse me?"

"These retreats are for swinging, switching partners, yes?"

Her mother had acclimated to western life so easily after moving to the US, but she was a little naïve.

"No. It's just a place where there are no children. You have to be eighteen and older for most of them."

"Oh. No swinging?"

"No. He just wants to take you some place romantic and relaxing. That's all."

"Hmm. No wonder he looked hurt when I yelled at him."

She bit her lip trying not to laugh. She didn't want to hurt her mother's feelings. "Tell you what. Go talk to Dad and make up. Jensen is up so we can chat about all the work we have to do."

"Hello, Mrs. M," he called out.

"Tell him I said hello."

"*Ma*ma says hello. Go find Dad."

"Okay. Make sure you relax."

"I will. Love you."

"Love you."

She hung up just as Jensen settled in the seat across from her. "So, what was going on with your mother?"

"My father booked a weekend at a couples' retreat."

"I got that much."

"She thought it was some kind of swinging couples' thing."

He didn't say anything for a second, then threw back his head and laughed.

"It isn't *that* funny."

"I just love that your mother has been in this country over thirty years and just does not seem to be sullied by it. She remains almost innocent."

"Stop talking about my country that way,"

He gave her what she called his little boy smile. It was lopsided and he rarely shared it with anyone outside of the family.

"Oh, you agree with me on some accounts."

She sighed. "Yes, especially when it comes to relationships. But then, my mother met my father after being in the US for less than six months. They were married three months later. Before that, she never dated."

"Your mother never dated? She was what—twenty?"

"Twenty-three. Remember, all she ever did was skate for Czechoslovakia. You didn't have a personal life then."

"She was singles, so no partner like you had?"

She nodded. "All right, are you ready to work?"

But as soon as she finished her sentence, Marta stepped out on the lanai, a tray filled with food in her hands.

"Ah, here is Marta to save me from the grindstone."

"We can work over breakfast."

"Only a heathen American would suggest that."

Marta set the tray down on the table. "Good morning, Mr. Jensen."

"Good morning, Marta. This looks scrumptious," Jensen said. He plucked something off the plate. "Scones. Brilliant."

Marta blushed on que. All women did that when he used that tone with them. It was what got them through so many negotiations, it worked when handling interviews, and probably got him more than one beautiful sub for the night. When she realized she had fisted her hand so tight around her teaspoon that her knuckles had turned white, Nicola pulled herself back.

What the hell was that about? But even as she asked it, she knew it was jealousy. Stupid, completely useless jealousy over a man she was barely attracted to. Okay, more than barely. A whole lot attracted to.

God.

"What's wrong?" Jensen asked. He had removed his sunglasses and was studying her.

"Sorry. Still kind of off from the flight over." She smiled at Marta. "This looks fabulous. Mahalo."

She smiled at Nicola. "Do you need anything else?"

"No, I think we'll be fine."

She left them alone. When Nicola picked up a plate and started to fill it, she ignored the silence from the other side of the table.

"Nic, you want to tell me what that was all about?"

She glanced at him, then back to gathering her breakfast off the tray. "What?"

"You looked ticked off."

She set her plate down and looked at him across the table. "Nothing's wrong, Jen. I said, I was just tired from the trip."

"No."

She frowned. "No? I did say I was tired from the trip."

To demonstrate it to him, she poured herself some more coffee. "See."

"No. You told me once you acclimate well. All the traveling for competition taught you how to deal with extensive travel. I remember it particularly well."

Jensen had one of those minds that never forgot anything. To prove his point, he had to tell that story. Again.

"We had just landed in LA three years ago—you remember, right after you started working for me. And I got sick. Stomach was all topsy-turvy and you told me to suck it up. You said you were a woman and you dealt with it. Learnt it from your days on the road as a skater. Remember?"

Of course, he remembered that. He remembered everything.

"How was I to know that you had food poisoning?"

He grunted but didn't continue berating her. Instead, he gathered up enough food for a small army and started to eat.

"Good appetite," she commented.

"I always have a good appetite. Well, except when I was using."

"Hmm."

He looked up from his plate and studied her again. "What's wrong?"

"There's nothing wrong."

"There is something off this morning. Did your night go badly?"

She shrugged. "Not really. Had a fabulous time. Serenity is expecting."

"Expecting what?"

She rolled her eyes. "She's pregnant."

"Oh, hmm. Is that your reason for feeling off?"

"Why would that make me feel off?"

"She's younger than you...and now having a baby. You know?"

"No. I. Don't."

Jensen was usually better at handling her anger. Granted, many times she knew he did it to get a rise out of her. Now though, he seemed to genuinely be acting like an asshole.

"The old baby ticker has to be ready to ring sometime soon."

She felt her temper rise. It didn't happen that often. In fact, Oliver had often said she was cold as the ice they skated on. When her temper got going, that ice could shatter.

"The baby ticker? Oh, right. All women are just dying to have children because we aren't real women without them."

"That's not what I meant."

"No?" She crossed her arms beneath her breasts. "Why don't you tell me what you meant?"

"I don't think I want to do that. And I truly don't like your tone."

"Then you shouldn't be such a total jackass."

Irritated with him and herself, she grabbed her coffee and rose out of her chair.

"When you are through with breakfast, I'll be inside working. Something I like to do...mostly alone."

She stomped off across the lanai and into the house. She was better off in the cool air of the house than dealing with Jensen.

JENSEN WATCHED Nicola as she made her way to the house. He had done it on purpose. He'd been raised better than to say rude things to a woman in the manner he did with Nicola. It was the only way to put distance between them. If she was angry with him, she'd be cool to him. No more fun banter, sexy smiles, and maybe—just maybe—he'd be able to fight this need that kept building inside of him.

He'd walked outside just a few seconds ago thankful that he had relieved himself of the tension that had been growing. All he had to do was hear that warm tone in her voice and the calm he'd created had slipped from his fingers in a matter of seconds.

One more glimpse of her rounded backside before it disappeared into the house along with every other luscious inch of her. With a groan, he shoved his hand through his hair. This was just not going the way he thought it would.

Worse, he felt like a perv. Nicola might forget it sometimes, but she worked for him. He was not some bloody sexual predator. It had never been his thing to seduce a woman who worked for him or for his company. It was just not done by Wulfs.

All of that didn't seem to matter because he wanted her. More than was good for him or her. He'd learned control, but with her, this woman who coordinated everything in his life, he couldn't seem to control himself around her. He was sure a psychiatrist would have a field day with that one.

He rolled his shoulders and decided he needed to buck up and be a man about it.

Now he just had to persuade his cock not to stand at attention begging for a pet every time he was in her presence and he would be right as rain.

chapter four

After their skirmish on the lanai, if one could even call it that, they settled into work without a problem. Nicola knew their one issue being there would be the hours. Their sleep patterns were off, and it left both of them cranky. She thought it might have more to do with Hawaii itself.

From the first time she had visited the islands, she had been in love. She could never live in the climate all the time. She still loved snow and cold weather, but there was something beyond special about Hawaii. Beauty surrounded you no matter if you were in the swankiest hotel or the humblest of homes. There was no denying that Hawaii had one of the most breathtaking vistas. It helped that her best friend in the world lived here.

"It's not like you to stare off into space."

She blinked and focused on Jensen. He'd behaved himself the rest of the morning, but that was how it went with him. She knew from his case history that he had acted out that way with drugs also. He'd get pissed and strike out, but the way he did it in those days was by getting high. Now he said inappropriate things. Most of the time he directed it toward other people, but lately, he'd increasingly zeroed that acerbic wit in her direction. And that led her to think about her future beyond the Wulfs.

"Nic?"

She shook her head. "Sorry. It's Hawaii. It makes me want to just lay around."

"Hmm, I can understand that. Something about the air I think. It's heavy and sweet."

She nodded. "So, you are ready for your meeting next Monday."

"Tell me again why you aren't coming?"

"Pool. Me. Not moving."

He looked over his glasses at her, and she was sure most people would find the move condescending. Instead, it turned her on. Heading into his very late thirties, the bad boy turned into the very naughty professor with those glasses on. Like right now as he gave her a look of disappointment. It made her want to do all kinds of naughty things to him.

"Instead of spending time with me on Maui, you want to sit here by the pool?"

"I also have a friend coming in on Monday from my old days of skating."

And, as soon as the words left her mouth, her phone vibrated on the table. She saw it was Jeff.

"Give me a sec." He nodded. She clicked on the phone. "Why are you calling me?"

"I love you, too," Jeff said.

"State your business or I'll hang up."

"I have to go back to the mainland, so I was wondering if we could meet up next weekend."

"I think I can find the time for lunch, especially if you're buying."

"Always the mercenary. Okay. We'll be there late Saturday. How about we do lunch on Sunday?"

"That sounds brilliant."

"Watch yourself, cowgirl. You're starting to sound British."

"Oh, bite me. So, next Sunday, around one?"

"Sounds good. Text me a place to eat and I'll meet you there."

"Bye."

When she clicked off her phone, she set it down again and looked up to find Jensen studying her.

"What?"

"Who was that?"

She wasn't accustomed to Jensen being so nosey about her personal life. He usually went on his way, doing whatever, and left her alone. Lately, though, he had become interested in whatever she was doing. It was a bit unnerving.

"Jeff."

"The bloke with the reality show?"

She nodded. "We were on the circuit at the same time. He was singles."

"Ah. And he just called you out of the blue?"

"Why are you so interested in this?"

He gave her one of those shrugs that irritated her. But she would not fall for it. She wasn't going to get into another argument with him before he left the island.

"Just am. I thought it odd that you're hooking up with him and you're in Hawaii."

"He and Ben are on Maui right now. They wanted to see me, but they have to make a trip back to the mainland for a bit, so we'll be meeting up next weekend."

He nodded but made no comment. Dammit. How did he do that? He could garner information from her even when she knew that was what he was doing.

"So, do you want to go over this family? I know that you like to have a background of everyone you're going to be dealing with."

"Sounds like a good plan."

Inwardly she sighed with relief. With a plan in place, she pulled up the information she had and started at the top of the family.

"First you have Robert. He's the patriarch and raised most of the people working in the leadership positions in the company."

"So, a bit like ours. A family business."

"Yes. And they are a tightknit family."

"I know that's why Mother liked them. They take care of their employees."

She nodded. Lillian Wulf might be considered upper class in English aristocracy now, but she had grown up poor. She had worked her way through college before gaining a position with Wulf Industries. She knew how important their employees were.

"Okay, tell me about the rest of them."

"Are you sure you want all of them?"

"No. Just the ones I have to deal with."

And that was what was important to him. Not that she faulted him for it. This wasn't a big merger in the whole scheme of things. In fact, it was one of their smaller ones. There was little money to be made, in fact. But for some reason, his mother was acutely focused on it, and Jensen was ready to make sure that she got what she wanted.

"Under Robert, his son Michael is Vice President. The two of them are very close. Then there is Lana. She is very important to the company, even if she doesn't have a big job title."

"Like you."

She glanced up at him. "Don't patronize me."

"I'm not. You keep things running smooth and that is very important."

"Well, thanks. Now, onto Sam. He's Michael's younger son. He's the manager of the resort."

"The one to blame for the problems then."

"Not really. His hands have been tied a bit. The family sustained some damage when Tropical Storm Gail came through last season. It was at a time when their funds were running low and they didn't have the capital to put up. Therefore, they had to borrow. Then they had a few problems here and there that caused even more issues."

"Problems?"

"They had always been known for having the best workers on the island. Their staff was praised. The other resorts did not miss that fact."

"They poached."

"Yes. Sam is well-liked, but he is seen as kind of a follower."

"And not good for running a company."

"Exactly."

"You said he was the younger son. Does that mean there is an older one still around?"

"Yes. Aleka."

"Interesting he's not in charge."

"He's not actually around. He left about thirteen years ago at the age of eighteen. There was a big blow up in the family, but I can't find out what it was about."

He blinked "*You* can't find out?"

"I know, right? I can usually find some kind of dirt. No

one will talk about them. Sent someone in to investigate. All I know is that there was a disagreement, Aleka left and joined the military."

"So, he left and went to war."

"Yes. But it tells me the family is very well liked. If they weren't, people would be ready to gossip about them. Even with the offer of money, people refused."

"Can you tell me what is going on inside the family that we need to worry about?"

She sighed. "Not much, but I do know that Michael and Robert do not want the merger. Sam does, but mainly because I think he wants out. The only bit of gossip I could get on the family is that Sam sunk a lot of his personal money into the resort."

"Don't all of them have a financial tie?"

"Yes, but he hasn't been that good with his money. While the other family members have invested wisely, he hasn't. Which means he will want the money. Robert and Michael do not. They want to keep the resort in the family."

"Which is exactly what we want."

"I know, but whenever a big company like Wulf shows up on the islands, everyone freaks out. Rightly so. Your family has no ties to the islands. Just remember, the heritage of the Hawaiian people was stolen from them."

"I'm not trying to steal anything."

"Still, they aren't going to believe you until they see an agreement. That's why your mother sent you and not your brother or sister."

"Why?"

She rolled her eyes. "You can be charming if you want to be. So, charm them. Let them know that you don't want to steal their resort and then they might believe you."

He sighed and shook his head. "I feel like a piece of meat. You still aren't going?"

She shook her head. "Alfie will be there."

"I don't like Alfie."

"He's your VP of acquisitions. Besides, I happen to know that you were best friends at Eaton.

"Are you still friends with any of your high school friends?"

She shrugged, relieved that they were finally finished with the work. "I didn't really go to school. I had tutors and took courses via correspondence."

"Ah, yes, the training. But you had to have friends back then."

"A few, but it was odd."

"In what way?"

She hesitated for just a moment. This was not like Jensen at all. He knew her history, knew her life before this. But he had never asked specific questions. "We were all competing against each other."

"It's like that in a way for all kids. Competing for sports, academics, all that."

"Yes, but it was more life or death. Plus, the competition was played out on the world stage. So many of us just don't even keep in contact."

"That's kind of sad."

"I guess I should rephrase that. The others probably do. I sort of had a stigma attached to me, so everyone avoided me."

"Jeff doesn't."

"No, but we were both outcasts. He came out early in life when it wasn't as accepted as it is now."

"You were both brave."

She shook her head. "No. I mean, Jeff was, but I wasn't."

"You walked away from a career you didn't want anymore. It would have been much easier to just stick around and get the endorsements."

If he only knew that it was more about survival than anything else, he would be stunned. As would most people. The story behind her departure and her ex-partner's suicide was so much worse than anyone could even imagine. And if she were honest, she missed the ice as much now as she did when she walked away.

"I guess."

He looked like he wanted to say more, so to divert his attention, Nicola decided to change the subject.

"What are your plans for the rest of the day?"

"I'm going to go over these write ups you compiled about the family."

"Okay. Just know that we have plans for dinner."

"We do?"

"Yes, the guys and Serenity want to have dinner with us."

He frowned.

"Stop. You like both of them and you admire them. I know you like watching their demonstrations at Rough 'n Ready; although, they won't be doing any more of those for a while."

"Oh, yeah?"

"With Serenity pregnant, they won't do many more of them."

"Ah."

"You don't approve?"

"No, it's their business. Not my job to approve or not."

"But you wouldn't do that?"

"Do what?"

"Give up that part of the lifestyle."

"I don't see myself doing that, but I have never seen me settling down with one woman either."

She didn't know why, but that made her feel incredibly sad.

"All right, you go over those dossiers and I'm going to start a little research on my own. I think once you lay it all out for them, they'll be okay with the merger."

"I don't like showing all my cards."

"Not normally, but there is nothing normal about this."

He grumbled as she gathered up her stuff.

"What time is dinner?"

"It's at seven."

"Good."

She turned to leave, but he stopped her with a comment.

"Are you sure you don't want to go to Maui?"

She shook her head. "I have some research to do here."

"And by research you mean..."

She sighed. "I don't want to go."

There, she said it.

"Why not?"

"I hate these things. I like the background research, and I don't mind getting dirty to get the job done. But I hate being there as your subordinate."

He looked at her over his glasses again, and she had to fight the little shiver that ran through her blood. Dammit, why was that so damned sexy to her?

"You hate reality?"

"Reality?"

"That I'm your superior."

"You are *not* my superior. I just work for you."

He rolled his eyes. "And?"

"No. It isn't how you treat me. It's how other men treat me."

He frowned. "How do they treat you exactly?"

"Nothing overt, but they always question anything I say. Not all of them, but I would say about ninety-five percent."

"Any other issues?"

Other people who didn't know him better would say it was a simple question. She knew the tone though. Quiet, unassuming...prelude to an attack.

"No. I did have to deal with that Jerry Obenstein in Texas last time, though. He apparently thought it was okay to pat my ass and suggest he prove to me just how much bigger Texans were."

Anger lit his expression. "What the fuck, Nic? Why didn't you tell me?"

"First of all, I can take care of myself. A well-placed stiletto to his toe helped, along with my *accidental* knee to his groin."

He blinked. "Accidental?"

"I played it that way. If he wouldn't have backed off then, I would have told you."

He grunted but didn't say anything.

"He wasn't too happy when I told him that contrary to his belief, from what I'd felt, not *all* things were bigger in Texas."

He blinked, then burst out laughing. "You have always had an understated dark side that I love, Nic."

She smiled. "Thank you. I'm going to grab a bite to eat and then make some calls. Do you need anything else?"

"No."

She gathered up her laptop and planner and headed out the door. When she stepped out into the hall, she drew in a big breath, then released it slowly. Why was he getting to her now? She had always thought of him as attractive. Most people would. There was a reason he was constantly ranked as one of the most eligible bachelors in England…well, actually, the world. High cheekbones, slim, toned muscles, and a darkness that unfailingly seemed to lurk in the background, which invariably attracted women. A bad boy to the extreme.

Funny, she was never actually attracted to bad boys. When she and Oliver had met, he had been sweet, a little unsure of himself. It was when drugs had taken over, when he had lost all of that sweetness, that she realized she couldn't love him anymore.

Walking up the stairs to her room, she thought about the differences between Oliver and Jensen. Both would be considered bad boys, but there was something to Jensen that Oliver either never had or lost somewhere along the way. It was one reason that she thought Oliver would never have made it through a program. His drug use had been about him. He wasn't acting out, he felt as though he deserved to do what he wanted. If she had been in a similar situation with Jensen, he would have gone to treatment after she walked out. Not that she would ever be in a relationship other than their working one, but if Jensen loved someone enough, he would do everything he could to get her back. Oliver had used his last act on Earth to leave a note blaming her.

She stepped into her bedroom and sighed. She couldn't get caught up with thinking about things she would never know the answers to. When she walked away, she had promised never to blame herself, and she wouldn't start now.

HOURS LATER, Jensen sat in his office going over the day. He wasn't really sure what was going on with Nicola. She seemed preoccupied, and that was the only reason he had become obsessed with her. Probably. Not really, but it sounded like the best excuse he could come up with—this week.

Still, there was something going on with her. The two of them couldn't get through a conversation without a skirmish. It was as if she were fed up with working for him.

Is that what that damned Jeff wanted? Was he trying to steal her away from him? Jensen knew the show had left him a millionaire with a cooking line, several bestselling books, and a new venture in gay travel. Or, at least that's the most he could find out about him over the last fifteen minutes of Internet searching.

Jeff wanted to meet up with Nic. Why? He could very well be looking for a PA to work for him. Nic might have started off as Jensen's sober companion, but she was now an important part of his work. The company would be hurt if she left. And he would be as well. He didn't know how to function without her around. He hated the two weeks she went on vacation. Oh, he had used a fill-in from his sister, and the woman had been fantastic. But she hadn't been Nic. And that had been when he started to act like such an ass. It was when he realized he didn't like being without her.

It had almost made him run to the nearest dealer. That scared the bloody hell out of him. He couldn't go down that hole again. The fact that Nic had become so damned vital to him, to his way of life, petrified him. When had she become so damned important to him?

Before he could get too morose, his phone rang. He looked at the number and cringed. *His mother.*

The day just kept getting better and better.

He clicked it on. He didn't have a choice. No one did when his mother called.

"Mother."

"Jensen. How are things in Hawaii?"

"Fine. Nicola and I just finished going over some information, and she's doing a little bit of digging on the family who owns the resort. How is England?"

She paused, and that wasn't at all like his mother. His father had always compared her to an admiral. Full steam ahead and never stopping until she got what she wanted.

"We have an issue."

"An issue?"

"Julienne broke off her engagement."

It was his turn to be silent. His sister was the good girl, the one that always seemed to do exactly as expected.

"She what?"

"She broke off her engagement from Gregor."

"When did this happen?"

"Last night. Nothing has hit the rags, but you know that isn't far behind."

He rubbed his temple. "Bloody hell. Did she give a reason?"

"No, and that's what worries me the most. She doesn't seem to care that they broke up."

"Are you sure? You know what she's like."

His sister was a competent businesswoman. Jensen never doubted that she would pull her weight. Emotions, though, were not as easy for her. It had been like that since their father died.

"I asked, and she answered."

"Mother."

"I know, I know. She hides a lot from us but pushing now would be a mistake."

"You're probably right," Jensen said. For all of his mother's failings, knowing her children was not on that list. She knew what made them all tick. That's why she was so good at controlling them. Or she had been.

"Do you need me to come back home?"

"I have been handling my children for thirty-five years."

Handling. Yes, his mother was very good at that.

"Right-o. But be sure to call and let me know what is going on."

"So, you are headed over to Maui next week?"

Subject changed, no use trying to get his mother to talk any more about his sister right now.

"Yes. I take it you talked to Nicola?"

"No, but she keeps an updated calendar we all can see. Are you sure you're all right, Jensen?"

He hated the concern in her voice. It was the same tone she used during his intervention.

"Yes, I am. The time change is still hard to overcome here."

"Of course. Well, is there anything we need to cover about the merger?"

"No. Nicola has it all ready for me."

"I saw that she rented one suite for the two of you."

"She's staying on Oahu. She said she had some meeting set up with locals, trying to ensure we have some support there."

"Hmm."

Again, the tone. Even when she didn't use full sentences or words, she could cut him to the quick with just a hum.

"I'll be fine, Mother. Is there anything else?"

"No, nothing. But a warning. Your brother is talking about jumping over there. He's in Los Angeles meeting with his agent and some producer right now, and he's been keen to see Hawaii again."

Bloody hell. "Okay. I'll warn Nicola since Jakob has a habit of just popping in at all hours of the day and night."

"Take care, Jensen. And call your sister in a day or two."

"Yes, mother."

"Goodbye.

He clicked off his phone and tossed it on the desk. This was going to be a bloody mess. He had made the Wulf's a household name with his antics. He'd been on every damned rag in England and America. Hell, he'd made a few rags in Japan even. And now, they followed the family's every move. This was going to be a mess.

"Was that your mother?"

"Yes," he answered, not bothering to look over his shoulder. He used to love to talk things over with her. Now it all felt awkward. No. Not felt—it was awkward. He didn't know what had shifted in the last couple of months, but somehow, he couldn't be in the same vicinity as Nicola without fantasizing about her.

"Is there anything wrong?"

"Julienne cut it off."

"Cut what off? Her hair? Surely, your mother isn't worried about that."

He turned to face her and felt the inevitable rush of excitement that came over him whenever he saw her. Damn. He liked the way Hawaii seemed to leave her skin dewy. Or was that his imagination? It didn't matter. All it made him want to do was lick her flesh.

Bloody hell.

"No. Her engagement."

Her face went blank for a moment, then her eyes widened, and she grinned. It was the grin he rarely saw, one that was filled with happiness and a carefreeness she rarely showed him—or anyone for that matter.

"Thank God for that. That's a bloody relief."

"You're not upset?"

"First of all, she's not my problem. You are. And secondly, I would hate to see her marry Gregor. Wet rags have more personality than he does."

"True."

"I felt she was marrying him because she thought she should."

"What do you mean by that?"

She shrugged and approached him, stopping in front of his desk. "You and Jakob always get to do what you want. But there are more expectations on her."

"What the bloody hell does that mean?"

She sighed. "Just forget it."

"No. Tell me." He softened the demand with, "Please."

"Your sister plays the role of the twentieth century English noblewoman even though we are a quarter of the way through the next century. She knows she's expected to marry well, even though your family doesn't need the money."

"Bullocks."

Her lips curved. "I know that. You know that. Julienne does not. She's always been the one who did what was expected of her."

"What about Jakob?"

"Yes, he makes your mother happy, but he's doing what he wants. I mean how many people get to be an actor, a board member of one of the biggest corporations in the world, and related to British royalty. If he wanted to do something else, he would do it without a thought of how the family would react. Your sister is not built that way. She takes being a good girl to an extreme even I can't understand."

"You count yourself as a good girl?" he asked, unable to hide his amusement.

"I was. On the circuit."

The fact that she mentioned her former life as a skater was enough to intrigue him. She rarely spoke of those years, even though he knew she snuck away to skate every now and then.

"Yes, but you weren't, correct?"

"I was, then I wasn't. That's a heavy responsibility, which could even drive a nun to sin."

Pain always tinged the edges of her self-depreciating humor. He always wanted to dig more, to know more about that time in her life. Something told him that his inquiry would not be welcomed—especially now.

"You are saying she was marrying to make everyone happy?"

She nodded. "Everyone but her. Although, I don't know if she really understood how unhappy she's been these past eighteen months."

He cocked his head to the side and studied her. "But you have? Why?"

"I'm not family."

He shook his head. "It's more than that."

She sighed and sat in one of the chairs in front of his desk. "I can identify with being thoroughly unhappy. The last two years of my skating career, I was probably heading into major depression."

"That's why you left skating?"

"One of many reasons," she said in that same voice she had always used for the subject. Four years, and she had yet to ever tell him about it; why the little girl from Colorado walked away from a definite medal at the Olympics. And, he wanted to know. He wanted to know everything about her.

Before he could ask, her phone buzzed. She looked at the caller ID and rolled her eyes. "The press."

"I thought you said it wasn't a problem for you."

"It's not," she said rising from the chair. "This is where I get to be rude to tabloid writers. I don't get to do that enough these days."

She clicked on the phone. "Marty, I thought I told you to lose my number."

Jensen watched her walk out of his office, and he fought the urge to follow her. He knew it wouldn't lead to anything. It couldn't. His life was perfectly structured and if he took Nicola to bed, that structure would be shattered into a thousand tiny pieces.

That was something he could not do again. It would lead to losing control, which meant drugs.

Jensen knew if he tumbled into that hole, he wouldn't escape alive.

chapter five

Nicola was relieved that she had been alone working until late afternoon. She'd ignored Jensen's mother and the five messages she had left. After dealing with Jensen, she wasn't in the mood to handle his mother. One of the things Nicola had learned during her tenure with the Wulf family was to have rules of engagement. Talking to Lillian Wulf, when Nicola was still frazzled by her son, was not a good idea. His mother would definitely know there was something going on.

When her phone showed that Julienne was calling, Nicola grabbed her phone.

"Hey, Jules. How are you doing?"

"I guess you heard."

"Yes, your brother told me."

A long sigh filtered over the phone. "Really? I thought Mother would get to you first."

"She's been calling, but I had my phone turned off to work."

Jules chuckled, but there no humor in it. "And you've been avoiding social media."

"I find that to be a good thing if I have no reason to pay attention."

"So, you think there is nothing to worry about?"

Nic rubbed her temple. She didn't want a headache, not when she was going to spend time with Serenity.

"There's going to be gossip. You know there's no way to avoid it, but I have a feeling that it won't be particularly bad. It's not like either of you were in the rags much."

There was a long moment of silence, which worried Nicola. The rest of the Wulfs always seemed to think that Jules could handle anything. That her silence meant she was okay with the good girl role. Nicola wasn't so sure Jules was happy.

"Do you think I made a mistake breaking off my engagement?"

Nicola didn't answer right away. She hadn't really liked Gregor. True, she didn't dislike him, but...he was boring. Still, doing something so abrupt was out of character for Jules. She didn't cross the street without two alternate routes. Ending their engagement after three years was not something Nicola thought Jules would ever do.

"Nic?"

"Sorry. What happened? What made you decide to break it off?"

"There I was on the morning of our three-year anniversary and six months from our wedding, and it hit me."

"What hit you?"

"I stared at him across the table at breakfast about a week ago and I thought, 'Jesus, what a bloody bore.'"

Nicola stifled a chuckle. Most people thought of Julienne as some kind of super human with no emotions. Nicola knew differently. She felt more deeply, but being the youngest and the only girl, somehow made her more acceptable as part of the Wulf Industries family. So, if she felt something, people rarely knew it. Nicola did, though. She had spent years doing the same thing, until it had almost been too late. Julienne also had a fantastic sense of humor. She hid it from a lot of people, and it was so dry most people didn't know if she was joking or being mean.

"Has it hit the press?"

"Of course it has. For someone so boring, Gregor sure did want to raise a ruckus about this. I didn't think he would have his feelings hurt so badly."

Nicola thought of it differently. Gregor was a lawyer with political ambitions and losing Julienne would damage his credibility. She would never say that to Julienne, though.

"Have you talked to your brother?"

"Which one?"

"Either, both?"

"I talked to Jakob. He gave me a thumbs up, so that tells you how far we went on that conversation. I've been avoiding Jensen's calls."

As if on cue, there was a knock on her bedroom door just before it opened. Jensen popped his head in.

"Have you had time to figure out what to do about Jules?"

"First, your intrusion is rude. Next time wait for me to answer."

He rolled his eyes. "Okay. Now, do you have an answer for me?"

She shook her head.

"Is that her on the phone?"

"Oh, bloody hell, don't tell him it's me," Jules said.

Again, she shook her head. "No. It's Jeffy."

"You are a horrible liar," he muttered as he marched across the tiled floor. It was then she realized he was shoeless. Jensen rarely went without shoes or socks, but in Hawaii, he went with the Hawaiian tradition of removing his shoes while indoors. Why it seemed to mesmerize her now, she had no idea.

"What?" he said.

She blinked and looked up at him. "Nothing."

"What's going on?" Jules asked. Before Nicola could answer her, Jensen took the phone from her hand.

"What the bloody hell are you doing calling Nicola?"

He was quiet for a long time while his sister answered him. His face told Nicola that Jules was not in the mood for her brother's judgment.

"Jules…"

More ranting from his sister. Jules was quiet, and she always did the right thing in public, but she didn't take any crap off her brothers.

"Fine," he said. He held her phone out to her. "She wants to talk to you."

Nicola took the phone. Instead of leaving like she thought he would, Jensen wandered around her room, then out to her balcony.

"So, I guess you didn't want to talk to Jensen?"

Julienne laughed, although, it came out a little hard and brittle for her. "Yes, well, you know Jensen. Ever since he got clean, he has gotten a little holier than thou about things."

"Did you want me to handle the media?"

"No. I have my assistant dealing with it. You work for Jensen, not me. I'm just doing the no comment thing right now. Although, I think David will want to run whatever we come up with by you first."

"Really?"

"Of course. The man is in awe of your press-handling

abilities. In fact, he wanted me to call you before it was announced."

"That would have been nice."

"No, he felt that I should get your approval about breaking it off. He is positively batty about you. Not as bad as Jensen is, but pretty bad."

"What do you mean by that?" she asked as she glanced in Jensen's direction. He was paying no attention to her while looking out at the ocean.

"Come on. We all know that you are his binky."

She blinked. "What?"

"Um, I thought you knew he had become a little dependent on you. If I didn't know better, I would have said he was smitten with you."

She sighed. "Don't speak such foolishness." Inwardly she cringed. When she was defensive, she often talked like a reject from an Austen novel. "My advice to you is avoid everything. Take the rest of the week off, and maybe the following week. At least work from home. That way you don't have to deal with the press. Also, tell David I'm going to shoot him an email with your favorite chocolates—"

"He's already got that covered."

"Well, he doesn't need my help then."

"I'm telling him you said that. Thanks for the support."

"No problem. And, just for the record, I thought he was a little boring too."

Jules laughed, this time sounding lighter than she had earlier. "Brilliant. Now can you talk our mother down?"

"I'll call her tomorrow. I have a feeling your mother is in bed."

"Oh, bloody hell, I didn't even see the time. That is one good thing about you being in Hawaii."

As if a time issue would ever stop a Wulf from calling

and waking her up. "You need to come over here. You know I don't like warm weather all that much and I love it here."

"Sure, sure. Night, Nic."

"Night, Jules."

She clicked off her phone.

"So, you thought he was boring, also."

She glanced at Jensen. "God, yes. I told you that before."

"But you never said anything to Jules."

She shrugged. "Whenever Gregor talked to me, I always felt like I was a passenger on the movie *Airplane* with Robert Hayes telling me his life story."

"You never showed it."

"I was supporting your sister then, as I will now."

"But wouldn't it be better if you just told her how much you didn't like him?"

"First, I've learned not to get in the way of any Wulf and what they want. Secondly, I didn't dislike him. I just felt he was too staid for her. Plus, he was interested in politics, which instantly made me suspicious of him."

He smiled. "True. Now, when are we meeting Serenity?"

"We're supposed to meet them in town at about seven. The guys had a job today and they need time to clean up."

"What is it that they do again?"

She knew he knew. It was his way of putting people in their place. While everyone else let him get away with it, she wouldn't.

"They perform in a sex circus."

He blinked. "What?"

"You know very well what they do. They work security, mostly for Conner Dillon. I want you to behave tonight."

"You are the only woman who says that to me."

"Outside of your mother."

He shook his head. "Be ready by quarter of."

"Oh, that's rich."

"What do you mean by that?"

"You are rarely on time because you tend to primp."

"I do not."

Not in the mood for a fight, she shooed him away. "Go on. I have a few people I can contact about this to make sure the press is handling it okay."

"You know Jules has her own personal assistant."

"One that is out of his league with something like this. He doesn't have the contacts."

"You're mine, not hers."

It was her turn to blink. There was a thread of absolute ownership in his voice that shocked her. "What?"

"You're my assistant. Not hers."

"Yes, but if I teach David how to handle this stuff, he'll be a master at it. Then, he can handle it on his own."

"Fine."

She knew from his tone that it was anything but fine. She just didn't have the time to deal with him today.

"Go on. I have work to do and I don't want to be late."

"Be that way," he said almost playfully.

Once he was gone, she grabbed her phone again and started dialing. She didn't trust Gregor to be discreet. He was boring and bland, but he wanted to be a big boy in politics. She just had to be sure he didn't hurt Jules in his march to fame and fortune.

With that in mind, she clicked her phone on, then called one of her contacts in New York. It was never good to let the press get out in front of your story. They liked to rip their favorite playthings to shreds. She had learned that from her own personal fiasco.

JENSEN STARED out over the lawn of their house to the ocean that lay beyond it. The last rays of the sun disappeared over the horizon, and he drew in a breath of the sweet night air. He had been all over the world, and he truly loved to travel. Hawaii was one of his favorite places to come, not only for the beaches, but also the serenity he found here. There was no rush to get ahead for most Hawaiians. Instead, they were laidback, in love with their culture, and always seemed to be happier than many places he had visited. Nighttime was the best in his opinion. Sure, the beaches and scenery were beautiful, but at night, Hawaii seemed like a dream.

"Day dreaming?" Nicola asked from behind him.

He had been trying to deal with the impact she had on him for four years. First, it had been irritation, then amusement, now…well, he didn't know what to call it.

"Jensen?"

He turned slowly, but it didn't matter. She always seemed to knock the breath out of him these days. Worse, she had no idea. She stood there with a simple smile curving her lips, as if she didn't have a care in the world. She definitely didn't know how much he really wanted to bend her over his knee and spank her. He fought against the shiver that threaded through his blood.

"Are you all right?"

He nodded as he inwardly ordered his body under control.

"It's not day time," was all he could come up with in response.

She wasn't dressed up. Nicola didn't do that on the islands. Instead, she was wearing what was a deceptively simple dress. Dark blue, with large white flowers on it, it was tropical in feeling but not exactly Hawaiian. The dress was long to her ankles, but there was nothing formal about it. It was a sundress made of gauzy material. Worse, she wore her hair down. She rarely did, but when she did, he had to resist the urge to touch.

"What?"

"What, what?"

She rolled her eyes. "Now I see why we have John driving us tonight. I have to give you kudos though for getting ready before me."

He cleared his throat and tried to get his wits collected. "I think the jet lag is hitting me this time."

"You *are* getting older."

He heard the playfulness in her tone and knew it was just their regular banter. Why he wanted it to be more, he really wasn't sure.

"You are a mean woman."

"I never said I was nice. Ready?"

He nodded and waved his hands indicating he would follow her. As he did, he reminded himself that she was off limits, and worse, didn't live the lifestyle.

But she would make the best kind of sub.

No, she wouldn't. She liked to be in control, and that was something he could not give up in the bedroom.

He pushed those thoughts aside and focused on the present. "So, where is it that we are going?"

"Side Street Inn. It's a local favorite."

She stepped outside, and a slight breeze caught her hair. He curled his fingers into the palms of his hands. He would not touch it no matter how much he wanted to feel the way the silky strands slid through his fingers.

"Good."

"And they have kimchi rice."

Nicola knew his favorites, knew almost everything about him. "Definitely good."

"Hello, John. You know where we are going, right?" Nicola asked.

"Nicola, Mr. Wulf," John said, as he nodded.

Nicola slid across the seat and Jensen followed her. Once the door was closed, she said, "That is one thing we have in common."

"What?"

"Adventurous eating."

"Ah. When I first met you, I worried about that. I thought you would be a dainty eater."

She threw her head back and laughed. It was one of the things he loved about her. Her laugh was always loud and filled with joy. You never had to wonder if she was laughing to please your ego.

"Never. In fact, I ate more when I was competing. All those calories I burned in workouts and practice. My mother would often lament that I would make them go bankrupt with our food bill each month."

"Both men will be there?"

She nodded as she opened up her purse and retrieved lipstick and a mirror. "Are you going to behave? There's no reason to be so nasty to the two of them. They really are excited about seeing you again."

He slanted her a look. He knew the men were bisexual. In fact, he had seen them perform at Rough 'n Ready, along with Serenity as their sub, last time they were on the island.

"I don't go that way."

She smiled. "Not *that* way, even if both of them have gone on and on about your cheekbones."

"Yeah?"

"The word Adonis was mentioned."

He could feel heat creep up from his neck into his face. Maybe in the darkened car, she would never notice. He had no such luck. After applying her lipstick, she closed it and tossed it back in her purse. Then, she looked at him.

"Jensen, are you blushing?"

"No," he said as he felt his face grow hotter.

"Oh, my. How interesting, but don't worry, they won't hit on you. They both have their hands full."

He said nothing about that, because he knew it was the truth. It was the fact that she'd heard the two men talk about him that embarrassed him. Worse, he wondered if she shared their opinion.

Knowing those were dangerous thoughts, he decided to steer the conversation to something more neutral.

"Anything new on the Jules front?"

A look of disgust spread over her face. "It seems Gregor has been peddling a story that she was cheating on him. Saying she's some kind of nymphomaniac."

Anger rose so fast it almost choked him. "Where?"

"Nowhere yet," she answered. "I've quashed it all and talked to David. It seems that Gregor is making a play for a higher position in the minister's cabinet. Breaking off an engagement makes him look bad, or so he says. Don't worry. I'll make him regret even trying to peddle that crap."

He smiled at her. "That is one thing I love about you."

"What?"

"Your mercenary heart."

She snorted as she looked out the window. "This is

nothing compared to skating. Besides, he did the one thing that will lead to his destruction."

"And that is?"

She turned away from the window to look at him. Her gaze steady and there was no humor in her expression.

"You mess with someone I love, I *will* ruin you."

She said it with no malice or anger. Just as fact.

"I would expect nothing less."

She offered him a small smile, then turned to look out the window again.

He felt free to study her then. These moments didn't happen very often. Nic kept herself busy most days, but in the few times he saw her like this, she seemed so solitary. It was something he could understand. He might have the support of his family, but they would never understand what hell he had been through. In that, he always felt the two of them shared a kinship. Leaving skating had been hard on Nicola. She never talked about it, at least not to him or in his presence. She shouldered her pain and never let it show. But he knew it was there. The fact that she never let anyone see it was awe-inspiring. And sexy. A strong woman who could submit…

Dammit. He had to quit thinking of her in that way. She was not a sub, and she would never submit to him. And, besides that, he could never give her up as his assistant. He wasn't sure he could run the business without her by his side.

He had failed his family once, and he would never do it again.

chapter six

Nicola sighed with relief as they walked through the door, arriving just a few minutes shy of seven thanks to the traffic. Oahu was a small island, but it always seemed to take forever to get anywhere. For a girl who grew up in a small town in Colorado, she never thought she would enjoy big cities. Still, the last few years she had grown to appreciate the vibe of the crowds.

Jensen opened the door and waited for her to walk in. She spotted her friends in the back, seated at one of the long tables. Serenity was waving her hands around like a goofball, making it hard to miss them.

"Does she think we don't see her?"

She chuckled. "She's excited to see me."

"Just you?"

"I know it's hard for you *not* to be the center of attention, but yes, me."

"You're such a prat."

"I wear that name with a badge of honor."

He couldn't respond to her hit because they had arrived at the table. Serenity stepped around Mick and Adam to give her a hug, then surprised Jensen with a big hug too. She could tell because his eyes widened slightly.

"I am so happy to see both of you again," she said.

Both men then hugged Nic and gave her a kiss on the cheek. When she stepped over to her chair, she noticed Jensen gave them both handshakes but didn't smile.

"You're going over to Maui?" Serenity asked once they were all seated.

"No, I'm not. Jensen is going. I thought maybe we could do a pamper day while he's gone. Sort of a present from me for the baby."

"That sounds fantastic."

"I still don't understand why you aren't going," Jensen said. His voice was light, but she detected his irritation. She was sure no one else would, but she knew him well enough.

"Because you don't need me, and I have a meeting with Fukasawa. He's very influential on Maui, so I'm doing some prelim work. Besides, I don't want to talk work here."

She knew he wasn't happy about it, but he just had to deal with it. She wanted a fun night out with friends. She didn't get many of those, as she felt she worked 24/7 for the Wulfs.

"Serenity is the one who brought up the trip to Maui."

"She was trying to pretend that she likes you."

"Hey, I do like Jensen," Serenity said.

"Sure you do," Nicola said with a chuckle.

"Either way, I know you would like Nicola to be there, but this way, I get to see a little more of her. Plus, I get to try out that wonderful pool of yours."

"You can use it any time you want, even if we aren't on the island," Jensen said.

She slid him a look to see if he was just saying that to get on Serenity's good side. It would be exactly like him to be extra sweet to Serenity so she might side with him on some of their arguments. Jensen could be the most manipulative person to get what he wanted, even if it was to win a petty fight.

"That's okay. I already told her she could do that."

He opened his mouth to argue, but thankfully, Adam cut in.

"I understand you had Dillon handle the security on that home?" Adam asked.

"Yes. I was impressed with his services. If we get this upcoming deal off the ground, I might have him handle the security systems at the resort as well. Security is one of the things I think it's lacking. They haven't upgraded in over five years from what I can tell. That's not good," Jensen remarked. "Do you two handle things like that?"

Mick shook his head. "We handle private security. We can handle tech stuff once it is installed, but neither of us are good with installation."

Serenity snorted. "Yeah, I changed their PC out for a Mac. They are still lost, and that was three months ago."

"We don't work on the computer like you do," Adam said.

She opened her mouth to respond, but the waiter returned to take their drink orders. Once again alone, Nicola decided to push baby talk.

"Do you have an exact due date?"

"March fifth is what they are saying."

"That seems so far away." She looked at Jensen. "You know you're going to have to deal without me in and around March fifth."

"We can handle stuff," Adam said.

"I'm sure you can," she said. "But I want to get my hands on that beautiful baby. They always smell so good."

"I didn't know you liked babies," Jensen said.

She looked at him. "Who doesn't? Okay, maybe some people don't, but I love babies. New life and all that."

"Don't let her fool you, Jensen," Serenity said. "She just wants to buy clothes and toys for the baby."

Nicola laughed. "That's true. Plus, his or her first skates. That baby *is* going to skate."

"See," Serenity said with a laugh. "She wants a protégé."

"Do not. Not really. But then, wouldn't it be cool to have an Olympic ice skating champion from Hawaii?"

Serenity shook her head. "You think you're going to get some kid to concentrate on skating when there are waves out there to ride?"

"Probably not, but it was worth a try."

As the evening progressed, Nicola got a sense that Jensen was relaxing. Most people wouldn't think the charmer of the Wulf family had such issues, but she knew better. When he was off kilter, she knew it was harder to deal with his addiction. As he talked soccer with the guys, she motioned to Serenity.

"If you gentlemen will excuse us," she said with a smile. Serenity stood and followed her to the bathroom.

"Good God, I had no idea Mick and Adam knew that much about soccer," Nicola said once they were in the bathroom.

"They really don't, but they assumed that Jensen would, and they wanted to impress him."

"That's worse."

"Yeah, it is," she said with a laugh. She picked one of the stalls and went in. Nicola freshened up her makeup while she waited.

"Is something bothering you?" Serenity asked.

"No, why?"

"You just seem to be on edge."

Since she was the second person to remark about her behavior, it gave Nicola pause. "Do I?"

"Only someone who knows you as well as I do would notice. What gives?"

Nicola waited for Serenity to come out of the stall. "Jensen thinks I'm jealous of your baby news."

She frowned as she washed her hands. "What a load of shit. You aren't jealous."

"That's what I said. Then he remarked that you were younger than I am—"

"Oh, no he didn't." She grabbed a paper towel and dried her hands. "Let's take him out back and beat the crap out of him."

Nicola chuckled. "Good. I thought for a second he might be right."

"Could it be the problem of finding a partner?"

Out of all of her friends, Serenity was the only one who knew of her lifestyle. Even before Serenity had met Mick and Adam, Nicola had confided in her. It wasn't so much that she didn't trust people. Okay, she didn't trust people. She knew it had a lot to do with her life in the spotlight and how painful the fall from grace had been.

"It might be. I've not been with a Dom since…Jesus, I lost count. Tokyo?"

Serenity's eyes widened. "That's been over a year. What's up?"

She opened her mouth, then shut it.

"Ohhh, you have a secret. What's the secret…tell me," Serenity demanded.

She sighed. "I'm having really inappropriate fantasies."

Serenity studied her for a long, silent minute. "Oh. My. God. You are having fantasies about Jensen!"

"Shh, Jesus, like I need him to find out. It's just every now and then, he uses a tone with me that gets me bothered. Like hot and bothered." When Serenity kept staring at her with no expression on her face, she panicked. "I think it's because I haven't been with a Dom in so long. I just need a good session to work the idea out of my system."

"Is he the only one getting you hot and bothered?"

"What?"

"I mean, what about Adam and Mick?"

"Jesus, Serenity, no."

"I think it has more to do with the man and your feelings toward him."

"No. We're friends—at best. There are times I'm not sure I even want to know him."

Even to her own ears her proclamation didn't sound all that strong.

"You could always try a night at Rough 'n Ready. See what happens."

She had thought the same thing before they'd arrived in Hawaii. Now, though, the idea held no excitement.

"Ah," Serenity said.

"What do you mean by that?"

"You don't want to do that. You want Jensen as your Dom."

"Do not. Why on Earth would I want that?"

"Talking like an Austen reject again. You are defensive."

Even though she was worried Serenity was right, she shook her head. "We better get out there or the guys will be worried about us."

"Tell me about it. Those two are being overly cautious about everything. Well, almost everything," she said with a grin.

There. That was what she was jealous of. Knowing there

were two men in the world who loved and adored her. Nicola would never begrudge her friend that feeling, but she wanted it too. Well, one man. The sad thing was that she knew it would never happen. She wasn't cut out for the *happily ever after story*. She had proven it with Oliver.

"What did I say?" Serenity asked, concern lacing her words.

Nicola smiled as she opened the bathroom door. "Nothing at all. Let's see if they moved on to cricket now."

With a hearty laugh, Serenity walked past her. "They've got such man crushes on Jensen."

As she followed her friend, Nicola was worried she was way past having a crush on her boss.

AS THEY WALKED out of the restaurant and down the street to the parking lot, Jensen walked about ten paces behind the women.

"I take it you don't need us to stop by," Mick commented.

"You mean while I am in Maui? No. The house is a fortress and knowing Nicola, she'll be in bed by nine every night."

Neither men said a word, so he glanced over at them. "What?"

"Nothing," Adam said.

"Is there something you want to tell me?"

"No. I just think it's funny how men always think they've figured out women, but we always get our asses handed to us," Adam said with a smile.

"True enough."

On their drive back to the house, Jensen couldn't let go of the conversation. "Do you have something planned while I'm gone?"

Nicola looked at him, but it was hard to see her expression in the darkened car. The streetlights were little help in that regard.

"I told you. I've a meeting or two, and then there's laying by the pool."

"Nothing else?"

"Do you mean am I going to have a party and invite all the kids over while you're on Maui?"

"No," he said, thankful that it was dark in the car since he started blushing again. This woman always knew what button to push. "The guys were cryptic."

"You mean the two men you were very suspicious of before we went to dinner? Normally, this would piss me off, but since I get two days of mostly hanging out by the pool, I will ease your mind."

She placed her hand on the seat and leaned closer to him. In this position, he could see more of her. Her hair slipped down and brushed against his arm and then there was her scent. It wasn't perfume. He knew it came from the lotion she slathered on her skin. Jasmine. Bloody hell.

"I am going to relax. It is going to be nice just to enjoy Hawaii for a couple of days this trip. We have only stayed a few days here and there."

"Okay." He was fighting dual urges. One told him to lean further back from her. She was a temptation that he was having more and more trouble ignoring. The other need coursing through his body told him to take one big bite.

Thankfully, she moved away from him allowing him to breathe again. Where was his control? Everything he had learned during his BDSM training had taught him to use his own inner strength to control his actions. One whiff of her lotion and he wanted to tear off that blue dress and plunge into her.

This was not good. It was bloody fucking horrible. Once he was done in Maui, he would definitely have to make a trip to Rough 'n Ready to work out the demons plaguing him. Nicola was too important to him and the family to risk an affair with her.

chapter seven

Jensen looked out the expansive windows of the **Mauka** Resort. It was a little drab outside, with light rain falling, but it didn't matter. It was still beautiful.

The massive pool was empty, but you could still see a few people out on the beach. He didn't blame them for braving the crappy weather. It would clear up soon, he was sure, and besides, it was Hawaii and no matter what, it was always beautiful.

This view, along with the massive acreage, were the top two reasons they wanted to invest in the resort. And he should be happy. Negotiations were going better than he thought they would. With half the family wanting the investment, he knew that he only had a slight edge. The other half knew they needed an infusion of capital to keep the place running. They weren't happy about it; but, in the words of Nicola, life didn't always make you happy.

Damn, he was missing her. She hadn't even come to the plane to see him off. He knew he wasn't being logical, but damn, he wanted her there. She was right. He didn't need her. But he wanted her there with a ferocity that truly irritated him. He could and had functioned without her before.

He watched Alfie's reflection as he made his way through the board room. He stopped beside Jensen.

"It's hard to tell what they're thinking."

He nodded. "Very stoic. I think we have a good chance though."

Alfie sighed. "I agree. They need the help, and I don't think they have another company offering our type of package. I thought Nicola was going to come."

"She's in Hawaii."

"No. I mean here."

"Oh, I thought she told you. She stayed on Oahu. She had some work that she could do from there."

"Oh."

His disappointed tone had Jensen turning to look at him. Nicola had been right, they had been best friends at Eaton. They came from different worlds. The Wulfs had a long history of being a silent but powerful family in England. Alfie Thompson was new money. It was odd, because if someone heard their last names, most people would think Alfie was twenty-fifth in line for the throne. Wulf sounded like some weird family name made up by an actor. Instead, Jensen could trace his family history all the way back to before the Norman invasion. Wulf had been Wulfgang, so after World War I, they had changed their name. Well, shortened it.

"How long are you going to be here?"

He had arrived the night before and now he was ready to head back. It was as if he couldn't go twenty-four hours without seeing Nicola. Pathetic.

"What did you say?" he asked Alfie.

"Sorry. Lost in my thoughts."

Alfie smiled. "Hawaii does have that effect on me. Hard to hold onto thoughts."

"Excuse me," Robert Johnson said.

He turned with a smile. "Yes?"

"We are going to need a few days to consider this option."

"Of course. I wouldn't expect anything less."

"We might have a counter offer."

Alfie opened his mouth to respond, and Jensen knew it would be negative. "Any response other than *no* makes me happy."

Robert's rigidity seemed to melt a bit.

"I understand you're staying on Oahu?"

"Yes. We have a house over there, or I would stay here for the negotiations."

"Why don't I fly over there next Monday? That way you don't have to make the trip over here again."

"Of course. Give Nicola a call with your details and we will be happy to get together."

He nodded and walked back to the rest of his family.

"Well, that's brilliant. Now I can head back early."

"Of course."

There was a thread of irritation in Alfie's voice that caught his attention.

"Is there a problem?"

"No, I just don't know why I'm here."

He waited until the rest of the Johnson family had left them alone.

"Mainly because you are my VP in charge of acquisitions and you wanted to come, remember? Or have you forgotten your push to have some time in Hawaii? Take the rest of the week to enjoy the island. Fly to one of the other islands."

"Sorry," he said rubbing his temples. "I can't seem to get used to island time."

"Sure. Well, I'm off to the airport. Do you need a ride over?"

"No. I think I'll take your advice and spend some time enjoying this island first."

"Good. Let me know if any of the Johnson family contacts you early."

"Of course."

With that, he pulled out his phone and started getting everything ready to head back to Oahu.

NICOLA TOOK a sip of her yummy lava flow and looked out over the rooms in Rough 'n Ready. One of the things she loved about the club was the ability to see some of the play rooms. The private rooms were even better, although she hadn't been able to use them. At least tonight she knew she was free. Jensen wasn't coming back until tomorrow and she had wanted to see her friend's club.

"I see that my wife made your favorite drink of the islands," Micah said, having to lean down closer for her to hear.

She smiled at him and motioned with her finger so that he would bend down a little.

"Your wife makes the best damn lava flow."

"I thought you would play tonight, given the outfit."

She shook her head. "Not really in the mood." The outfit was another matter. It wasn't even that, but she wore a mask. There was no need for her to be accidentally recognized there. Granted, she normally wouldn't excite most people, but if it were to get back to Jensen, she would never hear the end of it.

Truth was, it had been a long time since she'd been in the mood. Probably when they went to Tokyo last year.

"Is there something wrong?"

One of the great things about having Micah as her first Dom was that he was so intuitive. He knew just how far to push her. It was also one of the most irritating things now that they were just friends.

She shrugged. "Nothing wrong. I've just been out of sorts lately."

None of her friends in the life intrigued her anymore. Worse, she was comparing them to Jensen, or at least what she imagined Jensen's behavior as a Dom would be. After her talk with Serenity the other night, her worries had increased. If this wasn't just some kind of funk, what would she do?

"Can I give you some friendly advice?"

"Can I stop you?"

His lips twitched. "Stop ignoring your instincts."

"What the bloody hell do you mean by that?"

He shook his head. "I taught you well. Figure it out yourself, Nic."

Without another word, he turned and sauntered off. She cherished her friendship with Micah, but sometimes he was a real pain in the ass.

JENSEN HAD PLANNED on going home, but when he found out that Nicola wasn't there, he decided to head over to Rough 'n Ready. He stepped into the club, which was packed. It was spring break, or so more than one person had told him, and it meant a crowded gathering. The fact that there was going to be a demonstration tonight by well-known Domme Heather D made the crush even worse. He had gotten to the main platform when he noticed Micah making a beeline his way.

"How's tricks?" Micah asked.

He shrugged. "Got back from Maui early, so I thought I would come in."

But now that he was there, he wasn't sure why. He didn't even feel like looking for a sub. What he wanted to know was where the hell was Nicola? All he was told was that she was out. Probably with Serenity. Still, when he called her phone, she hadn't answered and that worried him.

"Earth to Jensen," Micah said.

He blinked. "Sorry. Obsessing over something at the moment."

Micah smiled. "Why not come up to the office?"

Without the burning need to find a sub, Jensen went along with him. He had never been invited into the inner sanctum, but he had heard about it. It wasn't that it was overly special, but he knew that Micah rarely invited patrons up to the room.

He followed the club owner up the stairs, then into the office. One wall was a floor-to-ceiling window, allowing a full view of the club. The wall next to that held a bank of screens showing all the public areas of the club.

"You know, I had the same issue you have right now."

He turned. "What the bloody hell does that mean?"

"You seem to be hung up on a woman."

He made a face and turned back to the bank of screens. The fact that he thought Micah might be right worried

Jensen. It didn't mean he had to admit it. "Not sure what you're talking about."

"Hmm, preoccupied, can't find a sub to satisfy your needs."

At that moment, he caught sight of a woman dressed in black. There was something about the way she made her way through the crowd that caught his interest. Her sassy ponytail swayed with each step, and there was something so graceful and familiar.

"Who is that?"

Micah walked up behind him.

"Ah, that's Kitty."

He glanced at Micah. "Kitty?"

"That's what she goes by when she's here. Kitty Cat."

He turned back and found her easily again. When she turned to face the camera, he noticed she was wearing a mask. Not that odd; although, it was more like something Cat Woman would wear and not the usual thing someone would wear to a BDSM club. The black latex pants and vest definitely fit the persona.

Beyond that, it had been months since a woman had captured his attention. The familiar heat sped through his blood.

"Is something wrong?" Micah asked.

"I feel like I know her."

"Hmm, not sure if you've ever been here together."

There was something in Micah's voice that caught his attention.

"You know who she is."

"Of course. She's a member of the club."

"Who is she?"

"I cannot reveal that."

Frustrated and irritated, he turned on the club owner. "What the bloody hell does that mean?"

"It means that I agreed to keep her identity a secret."

His gaze moved to the screen and Jensen followed his line of vision. She was making her way to the door, and he was going to lose her. Without saying a word, he rushed out the door and down the stairs. He had to catch her before she left.

He'd gotten close enough to see her again. Jensen continued to push his way through the crowd to get closer. Then he got a bit of a break. She stopped and set her glass on the bar and said something that made Dee, Micah's wife, laugh. The woman turned her head just enough that he could see her eyes—and he stopped in his tracks.

Ice-blue and cold as ice.

He had only seen that particular shade on one other person in his life. His world turned topsy-turvy. Pursuing her wasn't important now because he knew exactly where she was going to be spending her night.

Instead, he stood in the middle of Rough 'n Ready as his world fractured into a million pieces.

"I take it from the look on your face you know who she is," Micah said.

He kept his gaze glued to her until she walked out of the club. Then he turned to Micah. "Yes. And I want to know how long you've known her."

He sighed. "Let's go back to the office and I'll tell you what I can."

chapter eight

Anger and irritation bubbled just beneath Jensen's flesh. As he followed Micah back up the stairs, he flexed his hands over and over. It was one of his ways of dealing with stress. He wanted a fix. Anything, even just a shot of whisky would work. It was the first time in years he craved the oblivion that only alcohol or drugs could bring him. His entire body seemed to pulse with the need to get high.

No. It wasn't that. This was different. It wasn't the slightly sick feeling he had when he needed a fix. The anger was there, but there was also a bit of excitement. It was Nicola and the secret she had kept from him.

"Take a seat," Micah said.

Jensen continued to pace and ignore him. What the fuck did she think she was doing? Lying to him…making him think that she knew very little about the life. Of course, she did suggest it to him when he was having issues while she was his sober companion.

It might help you with your control issues. From what I under-

stand, you would be in complete control of the situation unlike in regular life.

Of course, she knew that. She was *in the life.* Worse, the fact that she could read him so well infuriated him.

"Wulf, sit down." This time he used a voice that was definitely not his easy-going club owner voice.

Jensen stopped and sat in the chair in front of the desk.

"I can't reveal everything about Kitty."

"Nicola."

"Here, she's known as Kitty. I can tell you we've been friends for about six years."

"Six years?"

He nodded. "She always wanted to keep the friendship a secret. *Her* choice not mine. Beyond the fact that she is indeed a submissive, I really don't feel right about revealing anything else. You need to talk to her."

"Bloody hell," he said as he pushed a hand through his hair. When he brought it down, he realized it was shaking. Anger was replaced with confusion. "I can't believe she did this and kept it from me."

"It wasn't any of your business."

He frowned at the club owner. "The hell it isn't. She's my...assistant."

Micah leaned back in his chair, a small smile curving his lips. "That's it? Your assistant? I have a hard time believing that's all she is to you."

"What do you mean?"

"You're mighty upset over her being a member of this club."

"And?" he asked in a tone that was just a bit defensive.

"You need to ask yourself what it means for the two of you. It will change your relationship since you're attracted to her."

"Bullocks."

"Really? Because you've come in here twice since you've been back on the island. Haven't even picked up a sub. Dawn and Donna were in here asking about you tonight. And let me guess, you aren't even interested?"

He didn't answer the question because he couldn't lie. He'd had a great time with both women last time he had been on the island. Now...nothing. Not one ounce of interest for either woman. And it didn't make sense. They were both amazing subs who liked to push their limits. He had anticipated seeing them again.

"I suspected as much." Micah leaned forward. "Listen, I was in the same position as you a few years ago. It will be much easier for you and everyone else around you if you just give in."

"There are issues. She works for me."

He grinned. "Yeah, that was one of my issues too."

It was then Jensen knew Micah was talking about his wife.

"I'm not marriage material."

"I didn't say it would end in marriage, but if you want her this much, you might want to step over that line. It might be good for both of you."

"I highly doubt that."

"Still, you will have to deal with the situation. Letting it go will just cause even more problems."

"Fine."

"Are you going home now?"

"Yes," he said, suddenly feeling tired. "I need a good night's rest."

"Better to deal with it in the morning."

He didn't know if he could wait until the morning, but

he decided not to argue with Micah. Jensen wasn't in the mood for more advice.

He made his way out of the club and texted John. It only took a couple minutes for his driver to arrive out front.

"Short night, sir," he remarked.

"Too tired and not interested at the moment. Let's make our way home, John."

Jensen slipped into the car.

"Of course," he said, shutting the door.

As they drove home, John didn't try to talk. A sign of a good driver. He knew when Jensen didn't want to talk.

Instead, he opened his window letting the cool Hawaiian night air drift over him. He had to deal with Nicola and this lie between them. He knew he didn't have a right to know everything about her life. She was his employee, like John. He had no idea what kind of woman John liked, or if he even liked women. Nicola was different than John, than anyone else in his life. She'd made sure he didn't step over that line, and the one time he did, she was there to help him through the recovery. Why hadn't she told him? She hadn't shared this part of her life, as if he wasn't good enough to know about it.

Nicola was secretive about only one thing: her last few years of skating and her relationship with Oliver. Or at least, he thought there was only one thing. She had been a submissive longer than he had been a Dom. That was why she knew it would be good for him and his control issues.

And why was she a sub? He would think she would make an excellent Domme. Hell, the woman liked to control everything in her life—and his. If anything, he knew it originated with that Oliver chap. Something had been off there, but since she wouldn't talk about those last few years, he never asked.

How was he going to deal with this? They would have to talk about it. He couldn't hint because she would divert any discussion of her love life with sarcasm. He would be forced to confront her. They might not ever have a D/s relationship...

Fuck, that wasn't true. He had wanted her before, craved her in fact. Now, it was going to be hard to resist at least one session with her. Hell, he was getting hard just thinking about it. It was wrong, and he didn't believe in shagging their employees. Still, this was different. *They* were different. It was complicated and there was nothing he could do to fix the issue. If she said no, he would go with her decision.

But at the moment, he wanted one thing: Nicola under his control and at his mercy.

A SOFT BREEZE filtered over Nicola just as she was waking up. She could smell the sea and flowers. She drew in a huge breath, then released it as she took stock of her body. Her head was clear. Just one drink these days was enough to make her sleepy, and that was why she had used a taxi service for her trip into Honolulu. Still, she felt great.

She opened her eyes and realized the sun had already risen over the horizon. For the first time in a long time, she dawdled in bed. Usually she was up and going right off the bat, but with Jensen still in Maui, she had little to do today.

She thought about last night. It had been fun to see Micah's club, but she'd hoped to make a connection, even if only for a night. But no Dom had interested her. She'd walked into that club and instantly started coming up with excuses why none of them would suit. Even as Micah had suggested one or two of them, she had reasons why the Dom was wrong for her. Too tall, too dark, too…American. So, she'd headed to the bar for a drink, knowing that kept her from playing for the night.

There was a knock at the door and she thought it would be Marta.

She pulled her covers up over her bare breasts, since she'd only slept in her panties.

"Come in."

When the door opened, she was shocked to see Jensen there. He was still wearing his blue silk robe and pajama pants, but his chest was bare. She tried not to notice the thin line of hair that bisected his abs, then disappeared beneath the waistband of his pajamas.

"Nicola?"

She forced herself to look up at his face. "What are you doing here?"

"I came home last night."

She blinked. "You weren't here when I got home for the evening."

"No." His mouth curved. "I stopped off at Rough 'n Ready."

For a moment, her brain shut down. He was at Rough 'n Ready? Shit. She cleared her throat.

"Is that a fact? Did you have a good time?"

Until then, he had stood near her door, but now he walked into the room. His bare feet made no noise as he padded across the wood floor.

"I did, in a way."

Her heart sank. And why should that happen? If he was occupied with another sub, she could get on with her search for a new Dom to play with.

"You found a sub to play with?"

"I guess you could say that, although I didn't get to talk to her."

Jensen settled down on her bed and smiled at her. She frowned. He was acting odd, even for him. He might come into her room, but he had never invaded her space this way.

"What do you mean?"

"Micah let me into his office last night. I got to see the whole club, and I saw one woman who particularly intrigued me."

She sat mute as he inched closer. She could smell the familiar scent of his favorite aftershave. It wasn't over-powering.

"Do you want to know what intrigued me?"

She shrugged, then after a moment nodded.

"First, it was the outfit she was wearing. She was dressed in black latex and wore a mask. Then, it was the way she moved. Very elegant. And I know only one woman who moves that way, mainly because she spent most of her life on the ice."

The bottom dropped out of her stomach. He had seen her and known it was her.

"Are you insane?"

"Maybe," he said.

"That was *not* me." Did Micah rat her out? She was going to read him the riot act if he did. Then she would tell Dee, who scared Micah more than Nicola ever could.

His eyebrows shot up. "Oh?"

"How do you know it was me just by the way I move?"

"I've known you up close and personal for four years, Nicola, I know how you move. I have also watched some of your old performances."

She blinked, surprised by that answer. "You've watched my old skating videos?"

He didn't move his gaze from hers as he nodded. "But that wasn't all I saw."

Nicola waited as he moved closer. The way he kept invading her space irritated her. "Stop that."

"Stop what?" he asked, his voice playful.

"You know exactly what you're doing, and I don't appreciate it."

He stopped and moved a little away. "I apologize."

His tone was sincere, so she accepted it with a nod. When he didn't continue on, she waited. The silence stretched, and she knew that it was a power move. She had been in the life long enough to recognize it. She had used it during business meetings, but for a man like Jensen, he would use it mainly for play. He was waiting her out and even knowing that, she couldn't resist responding.

"You said you saw something else that convinced you that this woman was me."

His lips twitched. "Yes, I did. By the by, are you naked beneath those sheets?"

"No." That was the truth at least.

"Back to your trip to Rough 'n Ready."

"I wasn't there. You *think* I was there."

He gave her a look of pity. "You can't deny me. I know it was you."

"How on earth do you know it was me?"

He studied her a long moment before saying. "Your eyes."

"What?"

"It was your eyes. No one on earth has eyes that shade of blue."

It took all her power not to cross her arms and stare him down. Of course, if she did that, she would probably expose her breasts. She sniffed instead.

"I doubt that."

Even though she knew it was an uncommon shade of blue, especially with her dark hair.

"No one I've seen lately. So, do you want to explain to me why you've been a submissive all these years and not told me?"

She wanted to keep arguing with him, but she didn't see a point. Still, she could gain some ground on him.

"I will but not here. I want to freshen up and get dressed first."

He cocked his head to the side. "Okay, but don't be long. I don't like to be kept waiting."

Irritation slipped through her entire body. He waited until she nodded. Then he rose from the bed and walked out of the room, closing the door behind him with a click. She fell back against the pillows, her head swirling with what had just happened.

Now that he knew she was a submissive, what did that mean for their relationship? He had never made any advances toward her before this. It was one of the things that had made their working relationship so wonderful. He respected her for who she was and what she did.

She grabbed her phone and hit Serenity's number.

It took three rings before her friend answered. "You hate me. Why do you call so early?"

"Because Jensen just invaded my bedroom and told me he saw me last night at Rough 'n Ready."

"What?" Serenity shouted into the phone. There was a mumble of male voices behind her. "Jensen caught her at the club. Go away and make me coffee. Go on."

"Kind of bossy for a woman I know is a submissive."

"Just like you. I'm okay with being controlled in bed, but I control my life. So, he caught you?"

"No. He saw me. He didn't confront me until this morning."

There was silence on the other end.

"Serenity?"

"Sorry. I was just thinking what his reaction was."

"Not sure, but I'm going to punch Micah if he was the one who told on me."

"Oh, he wouldn't do that. Right?"

She sighed. "Before now, I always trusted him. Kind of hard not to considering our history."

"Yeah. So how did he figure out it was you? God, you weren't in one of the viewing rooms?"

"No. First, I would never do that. I'm not that adventurous. He saw me on the security screen in Micah's office and said he recognized me."

"With your mask and stuff?"

"Yes. He claims it was the way I moved through the crowd."

"The way you moved?"

"Yes."

"Oh."

Then nothing. "Serenity?"

"Okay, don't get mad at me, but I've been thinking he's been sweet on you for a while. The guys are convinced of it too."

"What do they know? They're men."

Serenity snorted. "True, but it was the way he talked about you in front of them."

"I think your pregnancy hormones are affecting all of your brains."

Serenity giggled. "That or too much sex. So, just the way you moved? Kind of romantic."

"No, he also saw my eyes."

"That makes sense."

"Stop taking his side."

Another pause. "Nicola, are you okay?"

She blew out a breath and watched her bangs dance before answering. "I'm not sure. He wants to discuss it."

"Discuss what?"

"That I hid this for all these years."

"Your business. But I thought you did it the last couple of years on purpose. Like, you would be afraid if he found out."

"What the bloody hell do you mean?"

"Please, tell me the last Dom you were with? Or at least how long ago? It's been a few months and that's not like you, babe."

"I'm in a funk."

"Sure."

"Okay, so I've had a few...dreams."

"I knew it. You're in looooove."

Fear pressed a heavy hand on her chest, and she suddenly found it hard to take a breath. She closed her eyes. She would never make that mistake. Not again. Soon enough, her breathing eased but the fear remained.

"Nic?"

"I'm here, and you're insane."

"Why?"

"In love? I am not *that* stupid."

"Why, because you believed in the wrong man once?"

Exactly. "I don't have time to talk about Oliver, or anything else other than what to say to Jensen."

"I don't know. I'd definitely offer my body up to him if I were you. I've heard stories."

"What kind of stories?"

"From a few of the subs at Rough 'n Ready. He's considered one of the best unattached Doms."

Damn, Serenity just had to go and say that to her. Now, she would want to know. Of course, she wanted to know. She'd been fantasizing for months about it, and now...

"Nicola!"

"What?"

"God. Okay, I am going to let you go because there is coffee and I can smell bacon. Call me later and tell me what happened."

"Sure. Bye."

She clicked her phone off and then decided to take a shower. She was definitely going to take all the time she could before she had to face Jensen. It made her a bit of a coward, but there was one thing Jensen needed to learn: she was a submissive in the bedroom only, but not outside of it.

chapter nine

J ensen controlled his emotions—or tried to at least. He wanted to pace his office, but decided to concentrate on his work, which lasted all of thirty minutes. He'd heard the shower turn off ten or fifteen minutes earlier, and now he waited.

Why was he waiting? Normally, he wouldn't. As a Dom, he controlled the situation. But, as he thought the night before, this was different. *She* was different. Also, she was as affected by him as he was by her. She wanted him. He would never step over the line without permission.

"Marta?" Nicola called out.

"I gave her the day off," he said just loud enough for her to hear.

She appeared in the doorway to his office. She wore her hair slicked back in what he called her battle bun. It was the hairstyle she wore when she wanted to kick someone's arse. The only thing free from confinement were her bangs. The red sundress she wore was one he had seen before, and it was enough to drive him insane. It didn't show much skin, only enough to entice him. The soft fabric hugged her curves.

His palms itched. He wanted to follow those lines with his fingers, mouth…every single body part that would work.

"Why the hell would you do that?"

"Do what?"

"Tell Marta not to come in?"

"I told her to take the day off, with pay. We didn't need her."

"Please tell me the coffee I smell was not made by you."

"Why would you say that?"

"Your coffeemaking skills suck."

"I only turned the coffeemaker on, Marta set it up last night."

"Thank God," she said, spinning around and heading to the kitchen.

"Please, just call me Jensen."

He heard a grumble from her but couldn't make it out. She returned just a moment later, walked into his office and sat in one of the two chairs in front of his desk.

"So, talk."

He knew *this* Nicola. She manipulated a lot of their conversations. Most of the time, Jensen was okay with it. He knew she did it to move their work along. She almost always had his best interest at heart. This was different.

"I think you are mistaken about this conversation."

She swallowed her coffee. "How so?"

"I have questions, and they *will* be answered."

She frowned. Jensen didn't care if she was brassed off. She would have to learn to deal with his authority. When she said nothing, he took that as his cue to continue on.

"First, you've been a sub for six years?"

She nodded but said nothing else.

"And you knew Micah before you knew me?"

She nodded again.

"How?"

"We were both in the life."

He felt it was more than that, but he didn't want to push her just yet. They had no agreement. "But you never thought to tell me."

"It's personal. You don't tell everyone about your sex life."

"But I don't hide it either. Also, I hate to point this out, but you knew about my sex life."

"True, but it's different."

"Why?"

"You're my boss. I know you can't understand that, but it's different if I know this about you."

"That seems hypocritical."

"How?"

"You know everything about me, but I know next to nothing about your life."

"First, when I was your sober companion, I had to know all that stuff about you. And let's be truthful, you know a lot about my life. Hell, my mother sometimes texts with you more than she does with me. So you know a good deal about my life, just not this small part of it."

"Why not?"

"Okay, do you tell Marta about your new favorite sub?"

"I don't have a new favorite sub…yet."

Her frown turned darker. "What the bloody hell do you mean by that?"

"We'll get to that later. I just thought since you suggested D/s relationships to me, that you would tell me about your own experience."

"That would have been extremely awkward. I had only

been working with you for a year when you had your one setback. It's different now."

"And still you didn't tell me. Was last night your first night at Rough 'n Ready?"

"Yes, actually. I wanted to see Micah's club."

He thought back to the way she was dressed and knew she was lying. "No. You were dressed to play, but I saw a drink in your hand, so you didn't."

She shrugged. He wanted more than that. He wanted to know exactly why she didn't go out of her way to find a Dom for the evening. He was starting to suspect she'd done it a lot, all without him knowing.

"So, which was it?"

"Both. Once I got there, no one really interested me, so I picked up a drink."

That was the truth from what he could tell, but there was something she was holding back.

"What are we going to do about this?"

She held her cup against her lips and studied him. "What?"

That was the way she was going to play it? The woman really was a piece of work. Jensen had to hand it to her. She was always so controlled, and now he knew she was a sub, she was too wonderful to resist. He hated subs who gave over too easily, and from the way this conversation was going, Nicola definitely wouldn't be easy at all.

"This heat between us."

Something flared deep in her eyes, but it was gone before he could figure out what it was. "I think you are mistaken."

Every word was enunciated with precision. It was a direct challenge, and the Dom in him couldn't—wouldn't—let it go.

Instead of responding, he rose from his chair and walked

around the desk. He took her coffee out of her hands and set it down behind him. Suddenly, he grabbed her hand and yanked her out of the chair. Her eyes widened as he slammed his mouth down on hers. She resisted for a second or two…then she moaned.

Her eyes fluttered closed as she opened her mouth to him. Jensen dove in, taking complete possession. She tasted of the coffee she had just drunk—and surrender. He lifted his hands to her face as he slanted his mouth over hers. The moment he felt her tongue slide against his, his entire body lit up. She slid her hands up his back as he took a step closer. Her entire body was pressed up against his. He shuddered as need took over. He wanted her, now, on his desk. It had been years since he'd felt like this. The overwhelming need to conquer, to have her at his mercy.

He forced himself to pull back. Her eyelids rose revealing eyes blurry with passion. He couldn't find fault with her. His heart was beating out of control and his cock was standing at attention.

"Tell me now that there isn't anything between us."

She drew in a shuddering breath, then released it. "This is not a good idea."

"I think it's a brilliant idea."

Her eyes searched his as if she could find an answer to some unknown question there. "It will complicate things."

He dropped his hands but remained close. "True, we will just have to be careful. No play during work."

"I only listen to commands in the bedroom."

"Only the bedroom? I thought you were more adventurous than that."

She shook her head, but her lips twitched. "I'm still worried about what this would mean for our working relationship."

"We can handle it. Think about it, take your time."

"How much time?"

"As much as you want. Also, we can set a time limit on our…collaboration," he said. "Maybe for just the remaining time in Hawaii. That way we know there is an end date so to speak."

The moment he proposed the idea, he wanted to dismiss it. Another week was not enough with her. That is what had worried him. Nicola wasn't a regular sub to him. For months he had fantasized about her, about them together. Now, he was giving her permission to put her own time limit on it.

"Really? You'll agree to that? Sure you will. You are never around long enough to form a long-lasting relationship."

They had a relationship…a friendship of sorts. She had seen the ugly side of him, especially after his one fuck up, but she still stayed around. Nicola didn't judge him, she supported him. If he fucked that up, he would never forgive himself. Even acknowledging that, he could not just walk away.

"You admit to wanting me as much as I want you."

She pulled her bottom lip between her teeth. It was a gesture he hadn't seen, except in the old clips of her skating days.

"Yes, but—"

His phone rang, and he couldn't ignore it. It was his mother and she would just call Nicola.

"This isn't over."

She nodded. Jensen swooped in for another kiss before he released her.

"You know you may not get your way," she said.

He smiled over the term 'may not'. "But what fun we will have during the process."

"I did not say yes."

"You also did not say no."

The ringing on his phone stopped. A second later, Nicola's phone started to ring.

"Call your mother. I am not in the mood."

With that, she turned away from him and walked out the door. As he watched her disappear around the corner, he almost sighed. It wouldn't be easy, but it was definitely going to be enjoyable.

NICOLA FOUND the rest of the day almost unbearable. They had work to do, and while she wanted to just roll up in a ball in bed, she had duties to attend to. The worst thing about it was that Jensen seemed completely unaffected about the earlier kiss. She couldn't concentrate and found her mind wandering back to the way she felt afterwards. Men had come and gone, but even her first kiss hadn't made her dizzy like the kiss from Jensen. Even as they went over figures and information about the Johnson family, she couldn't keep from looking at his lips. She could just imagine them as he kissed down her spine…

She consciously pulled herself away from that image.

"I think you need to call Robert. He might not be running everything now, but he's still the patriarch of the family. He will see it as a sign of respect."

"Very important to Hawaiians," he said, without looking up at her.

"If there is nothing else, I need to make some phone calls.

He glanced up over those stupid reading glasses. Dammit, her panties were already damp, and it was getting worse.

"Sure."

As she walked out of his office, she felt his gaze burning into her back. She hurried up the stairs to her room. She closed the door and leaned against it. Closing her eyes, she told herself that it was because she hadn't had a man in months—even though she knew it wasn't true. No man had ever been able to make her forget the entire world around her. Even the best of Doms hadn't been able to, and she had had a lot of them.

Her eyes shot open. Speaking of Doms, she grabbed her phone and called Micah.

He picked up on the second ring. "I was wondering when you were going to call me."

"Really? Like maybe a heads up would have been nice."

"I thought you two should work it out on your own."

"No, this is about Doms sticking together."

There was a pause.

"Nic, are you okay?"

"Of course."

"You don't sound normal."

"What the bloody hell does that mean?"

He chuckled. "Well, you're yelling at me, and you never do that. Even with people you don't like, and I think you still kind of like me."

"I might change my mind."

"Come on, Nic, you both needed a nudge."

"Giving you permission to tell him who I was?"

"No. He figured it out."

She snorted.

"I promise. On that little screen, he watched the way you moved and then he ran out the door."

She walked over to her bed and sat down. "That's what he said."

"In my experience, if a man is that obsessed about a woman, he's interested in more than a working relationship."

"Oh, believe me, he told me that this morning."

"Terms?"

"We haven't talked much about those, but he did say something about ending when we left Hawaii."

It was Micah's turn to snort. "Yeah, sure."

"What does that mean?"

"Nothing. You two seem attracted to each other, so why not enter into an agreement? Is there something else stopping you?"

"Work. We would have to deal with each other afterwards."

"That hasn't been a problem before. You and I have no issues."

"You're special."

"Aw, that's sweet. What about that attorney in Hong Kong you told me about? You were working with him, and I am sure you continue to deal with him upon occasion."

Dammit. One of the things that was wonderful about Micah was his intuitiveness. It was occasionally also one of the more aggravating aspects.

"True, but it's different with Jensen."

"Why?"

Because I might just be in love with him, and if it goes wrong, I'll be beyond screwed up.

She didn't say that though. She couldn't, because if she said the words out loud, they might come true.

"I don't see him every day. I also live with Jensen. Granted, the houses are usually huge, but still."

"Hmm. So you don't want to talk about it?"

Dammit.

"No. I don't know."

"Come on, Nic. You're smart. What does he have that all of those other men didn't? I remember asking you to come to Hawaii when I started my club and you turned me down flat."

"And you should thank me for that. Dee is the only woman who could put up with you."

"True. Still, you hold back from men all the time. Why is this man getting under your skin?"

"What do you mean?"

"Any other Dom of his caliber and you would say yes on the spot."

"I told you. Work."

He sighed. "I see you aren't going to be honest with me."

Guilt nudged at her. "I just haven't worked through all of it yet."

"Okay, but at least keep the option open. You two could be great together."

"Or we could destroy a great working relationship."

"If there is no risk, it's just not worth it to try."

She knew he was talking about his relationship with his wife Dee.

"Kiss that sweet wife for me and those babies. I have things to think about."

"Sure thing. Call anytime."

"I was nice. I could have called at six this morning, so behave yourself from now on, or I will."

She hung up on his sputtering. The call made her feel even worse about the situation. She was ready to say no. She wanted him, but it wasn't until this moment that she realized how much she valued his friendship. Nicola planned on leaving his employment someday, but she always thought they would remain friends.

Her phone buzzed in her hands. When she saw Serenity's face on the screen, she knew she couldn't avoid her.

"What do you want?"

"I was calling to see what went on today."

"Well, he proposed we enter into an agreement."

"Not surprised he did."

"Until we leave the island."

She snorted. "Yeah, right."

"Why does everyone have that reaction?"

"Who else did you talk to? You told someone before you told me?"

"Calm down. I had to call Micah and find out what he told Jensen."

"I guess I can deal with that. Okay, what's the plan?"

"I had planned on saying no."

"But?"

"That was before he kissed me."

"What?! Did you tell Micah about that too? I swear, you really—"

"Calm down. I didn't tell him."

"Good." Then she sighed. "How was it?"

"Talking to Micah? Same as always."

"Nicola!"

"Okay, it was hot, wet, and I couldn't think straight for at least half an hour."

"I knew it. You *have* to say yes."

She rolled her eyes. Serenity still had daydreams and fantasies in her head. She claimed to be a realist, but she wasn't. Not really. She was still the child star who dreamed of a happier life. At least she had it now with her guys. Serenity just couldn't understand that not everyone got a happily ever after.

"No, I don't. There are complications. Think about that."

"Like what complications?"

"Like I work for him."

"And?"

"That's…well that could be bad. I mean, what happens if things go wrong? Think about how awkward it will be if one of us is ready to end it and the other isn't?"

"Oh, honey, you're in love with him."

She fell back on her mattress and silently cursed best friends. "No. Maybe. I don't know."

"If you are, you're worried that after you leave the islands, he'll just be back to being a Dom with others and you'll be left out there on your own."

Her heart sank. "Yeah. Oliver was hard enough to get over. And he sucked as a boyfriend. I know Jensen is an excellent Dom."

"It's more than that and you know it."

She wanted to deny it, but she knew she couldn't.

"Remember when I was trying to figure out what to do about the guys?" Serenity asked. "You told me to take a chance. You need to take a chance again. It's been years since you've had a relationship."

"I have relationships all the time."

"You have sex. Albeit probably good sex, but not relationships. Those take time."

"We have ten days left here."

"And you have known him for four years. It will mean more." She paused. "Unless you are a coward."

"Don't even try that with me, woman."

"Why not? It works. Just think about it in the context of trying something new. You need to challenge yourself. I think your issue lately—which you have complained to me about—is that you find a lot of Doms boring right now.

Maybe you need to try for a deeper connection. Maybe you and Jensen can find that."

"Okay. I have to go now."

"Why?"

"I have a lot to think about."

Serenity laughed. "You do. Ta."

Nicola clicked off her phone without responding.

Could she do this? Jensen had become an integral part of her life in the last four years. Jules had called her his binky, but there was a part of Nicola that understood it went both ways. They had lived in each other's pockets almost from the beginning. Her attraction had started about a year earlier —surprising and embarrassing her. She couldn't pinpoint the moment she started thinking of him differently, but he had started invading her dreams. And there were those moments when he would smile at her. Nicola swore her heart melted right then and there.

She thought through the pros and cons. And she arrived at one definite decision.

Before she could change her mind, she hurried out of her room and down the staircase. She arrived at Jensen's office. He looked up at her—still wearing the reading glasses—and smiled.

Yep, there it was again. Her heart melted. "No work time play."

"Understood."

"We do not tell your family, and we keep this between us."

He nodded. "No need to get them involved."

"Then, I agree."

chapter ten

F or a long moment, Jensen said nothing. His brain had stopped working the moment she said the words 'I agree'. He blinked a few times trying to force himself to think, but his thoughts were still frozen. Did she really agree to be his submissive? Bloody hell.

She cocked her head to the side. "Jensen, are you okay?"

He nodded, then cleared his throat. All of a sudden he felt like an untried virgin. She was studying him as if she thought he'd lost his mind. Not exactly the reaction he wanted from his submissive.

He wanted this, needed it on a level that he didn't yet understand. She was standing there, the bright sunlight shining behind her, and he had only two words running through his mind.

I want.

He wanted her on his desk, bent over as he took her from behind. He wanted to lean back in his chair while she was on her knees in front of him, his cock in his mouth. He could just imagine the way her tongue would swirl around his shaft as she gazed up at him with those damned eyes of hers.

Damn. Beads of sweat had already dampened his palms. She left him randy and almost out of control in his need for her. They had a verbal agreement. It was still work hours. He knew it was important to stick to their agreed upon rules, but he wanted a taste of her. No matter that he had waited for months. Now that he knew she was going to submit, it was hard to resist the pull of her. She was such a strong woman, so he knew their D/s play would be challenging.

"Tonight then?" he asked.

She nodded.

"Do you want to go to Rough 'n Ready?"

The moment the question slipped out, he regretted it. He didn't want to share her with anyone else. Even if that meant walking around a club, he didn't want people to look at her, to think about her. She was his.

And he sounded like a boy with a new toy. Bloody fucking hell. It was the first time in his history as a Dom that he felt so possessive with a sub.

"No," she said. "This is us, alone. I don't want an audience."

He felt the same way, but he thought she might want to get a private room. He wasn't stupid enough to make the mistake a second time.

"Do you go to many clubs?" he asked.

She hesitated. He wondered at it, and he really didn't want to order the answer out of her. Thankfully, she said, "I did years ago, but I stopped."

"Why?"

"Truth is, I didn't want to run into you at any of them. You are a member of several of the clubs I frequented. I thought it would be odd to run into each other, even if you knew of my preferences."

"That worked out well," he said, not bothering to hide the sarcasm in his voice.

Her mouth twitched. "You weren't supposed to be there, if you remember."

Jensen shook his head. "So sneaky. That's why you dressed up the way you did?"

"I'm still recognizable. My worry is that it would reflect on the family if I were found there. Micah's pretty tight with security, but you never know. Those rags have some incredibly sneaky bastards working for them. And while it's okay for you to be a member, they would rip me to shreds for the fact that I am woman."

The way she talked about Ross made him itch. "I sense there's something more between you and Ross."

She frowned. "Are you talking romantically? There isn't. He's in love with his wife."

Jensen knew that was true, but there was something else there, something that told him they had a deeper connection than just two people in the life. He knew she was. Granted, Ross was the owner of the club, but Jensen knew a lot of club owners wouldn't allow it. That meant they had a more personal relationship.

"I also heard two subs complaining about him and the other owner. They do no demonstrations or play unless it's with their wives."

"Yes, I've heard that too. Have you ever played publicly?"

He shook his head. "I didn't want to create more grief for you. Have you?"

She wrinkled her nose. "I had to perform for so many

years on the ice, I wasn't inclined to do so in my private life."

That made sense. He knew she still loved to skate, but only did it if she could rent some time on the ice, privately. She hated being gawked at. Even after all these years, people who loved skating recognized her. More than once they had been stopped for autographs, especially when they were in Colorado.

He glanced at the clock. It was late afternoon and he knew that they both needed to eat. They would need it for the activities he had planned for them. "Did you want to go out for dinner?"

She thought about it. "I guess we could. There isn't much to eat since Marta wasn't here today."

"Where?"

"How about that little sushi place down in Waikiki near the hotels."

He liked that idea. It was always busy, but the sushi chefs were always fast. It would be filled mainly by locals.

"That sounds brilliant. I have an errand to run, but I'll be back in about an hour or so, then we can go. Does that work?"

She nodded and said nothing else before leaving the room. He turned his seat around to stare out the window. He had fought this need for her for months and now he was giving into it because she was a submissive. The idea that she worked for him apparently didn't bother him as much as her not living in the life. Now that he knew she was, he could care less about the work relationship. No, that was wrong. He did care. He needed her. He had never had a personal assistant who was as good at knowing what he wanted and exactly when he wanted it.

He shook himself out of his thoughts and knew he had to

get a move on. He had to call Micah to see if he was at the club, so he could do some shopping. Jensen needed some toys to play with tonight and they had the best supply.

He dialed the number to the club and Micah picked up on the second ring. "Rough 'n Ready."

"Ross, this is Wulf. I was wondering if you could do me a favor and let me come in to shop now."

"Not coming to the club tonight?" Micah asked, humor threading his voice.

"Nope. I have a very private night planned."

"I thought you might. Come on in. I'll be happy to let you spend money at my club."

Jensen hung up and grabbed the keys to the sedan they had rented. The sooner he got this and dinner done with, the sooner he would finally have Nicola all to himself.

chapter eleven

They arrived home just as the sun was setting. Jensen had driven, and Nicola assumed that he had told John to make himself scarce. Hopefully, he had used some kind of excuse as not to raise suspicions. There was no need for rumors to start when this affair would be short-lived.

She and Jensen walked side-by-side as they made their way to the front door. The idea of what was to come had left her very aroused and a little scared. What if they didn't work well together? It happened sometimes, and usually she could merely walk away. If tonight was a disaster, it would lay there between them, through the next few days at least.

He unlocked the doors and shut off the alarm. After she stepped through the threshold, he shut the door behind her, then locked it. Her heart raced as she knew each step further into the household was a step closer to their time together. During dinner, she'd forced herself to eat even as her body had begged for relief.

She'd just slipped off her shoes and was starting to make her way to the kitchen when he said, "Nicola."

His voice had changed. It wasn't something people would normally hear, but she knew him well. It was deeper, a bit more authoritative than she was accustomed to. This had to be his Dom voice. "Yes?"

"What kind of panties are you wearing?"

Really damp ones. "A thong."

"Go upstairs and strip out of your clothes but leave your panties on. Sit on that little bench in front of my bed, legs spread, hands behind you. Do you understand?"

She nodded.

"Oh and take down your hair. I like it down. Go."

She wanted to defy him, just to see what he would do. It might cause a few sparks, but that would delay their fun. Nicola so wanted to have fun.

Without rushing, she walked up the stairs to his room. Just because she was doing his bidding, it didn't mean she had to rush. In fact, taking her time would draw out the anticipation just a little more.

His room was a bit bigger than hers, but with the same sized bathroom. She glanced at his dresser. On it lay several toys to play with and she wondered about them. Before she could inspect them closer, he apparently didn't trust her to follow his orders.

"Don't dawdle," he yelled up at her.

She stripped out of her dress, followed by her bra. She folded them and put them on the bench where she was to sit. As instructed, she pulled the pins out of her hair. When she heard his footsteps on the stairs, she hurried over to the bench and sat as he had ordered.

Even though she still wore her panties, she felt exposed. Her breasts were bare, and there was no mistaking the dampness in her panties. He would definitely be able to see it with her in that position.

He walked through the door carrying a tray that had a water pitcher and two glasses on it.

"Well, you do make a very good sub. Who would have known?"

He set the tray on the dresser, then approached her. He stopped between her legs.

"I had a feeling you would have pretty breasts, and I was right," he said as he brushed the backs of his fingers over one nipple. His touch was like a shockwave to her system. Heat sparked, and her nipples tightened.

She wanted more, craved it, but she did not utter a word. He stepped away and she almost moaned in irritation. He made his way to the balcony.

"I know it will probably make it hot in here, but I need to close these doors. People know we live here, and you know how high-powered lenses can wreak havoc on privacy."

She nodded.

When he had them closed, he walked back over to her. "We haven't talked much about what you have done in the past. I assume regular play, yes?"

"Yes."

"I have a feeling that you might like spanking." She nodded. He hummed, and it seemed to vibrate through his body. "Have you ever participated in rope play?" he asked, as he started to unbutton his shirt.

"Yes."

"Breath play."

"Absolutely not."

His mouth curved. "Me either. I tempted death a few too many times to play with that."

He dropped his shirt on the floor and then undid his belt and removed it. Her nipples tightened even more as anticipation wound through her body.

He stepped up closer to her again and slipped his finger beneath her chin. He waited until she made eye contact.

"There is one thing you need to understand," he said. His tone turned rougher when he next spoke. "I own your pleasure, Nicola. Every sigh, every moan, every release. They. Are. Mine. Do you understand?"

"Yes."

He nodded and stepped away again. Dammit, he was killing her by drawing this out. Usually, she thrived on it, and she normally would be happy to let her Dom take his time. Tonight, each move he made left her more aroused. He didn't even have to touch her. Just the thought of what was next had her ready to scream.

He was facing away from her, but she could see in the dresser mirror that cocky little smile curving his lips. Jensen knew exactly what this was doing to her.

"I went to the club today and Micah allowed me to shop before they were opened. I had to guess at what you liked, but maybe we need to pick up some rope tomorrow. I do like to tie up a woman and make her come."

She shivered, her breasts swaying with the motion. Her reaction caught his attention, which was reflected in the mirror, was another turn on. He raised his gaze to hers and the heat she saw in his eyes added another layer of arousal. A Dom who could control himself this well was a force to be reckoned with. He was also going to probably show her the time of her life.

"All right, I settled on a few spanking toys and vibrators. Of the toys, which do you prefer?" he asked turning around. In one hand he held a wide paddle. The other, a flogger.

"I like both, but the flogger is what I would prefer."

He smiled. "Amazing that you make such a good sub. I never would have believed it, but...well, let's not go into that right now." He set the paddle down, then grabbed something else. When he made his way to her, she noticed it was a vibrator. He set the toys on the bed, then stepped in front of her again. "What is your safe word?"

"Iris."

"You may move your hands to the front now." He rubbed her shoulders, relieving some of the tenseness. Another sign of a good Dom. "I know it goes without saying but tell me if you have any discomfort. Not to the level of a safe word, but just uncomfortable. Don't want to strain your muscles."

She nodded.

"Normally, I wouldn't care if you called me Jensen or Sir. I think it be would best if we use Sir during play."

It was a way of separating their working and personal relationships. She didn't normally go for the idea, but somehow it fit Jensen.

"Yes, Sir."

He chuckled, the sound dancing over her nerve endings.

"I think that's the first time you have ever called me Sir. Now take off my pants."

Nicola unbuttoned then unzipped his pants, slipping them down his legs. She was a bit disappointed that he was wearing a pair of knit boxers. His erection strained against the soft fabric. He stepped out of them and she picked them up. After taking them from her, he folded the pants and placed them on the dresser.

He caught her gaze as he walked back to her. She didn't like Dom's who ordered a woman not to look at him. There had been one in her past that told her to stare at the floor. She told him to fuck off and left. They were definitely not compatible.

But here with Jensen, she felt comfortable. It was almost as if they understood each other on this level, which made no sense. Their public lives were totally different from this. She felt in sync with him more so than Akito one of her favorite Doms. Nicola had a feeling that none of them were going to compare to Jensen.

He took her hands and said, "Stand up."

She did as he ordered, then waited. It was apparent that Jensen was the type of Dom who liked to draw things out. Her heart pounded against her chest as she tried to control her breathing. What would he do next, or have her do? They hadn't even really started, and she was so damned wet. Just the thoughts that were running through her head about what would come next.

He walked up behind her.

"What is going on in that head of yours, Nicola?" he said, his breath against her ear.

"Nothing, Sir."

He slapped her ass. It was barely a slap, but the heat of his palm against her flesh sent a fresh wave of arousal low in her belly. Jesus. "That's for lying to me. Tell me."

"I like that you don't mind me looking at you or making eye contact."

He rested his chin on her shoulder. His breath feathered over her neck. "Some Dom's don't like that, I take it?"

She nodded.

"I will never understand some people. I'm sure that some subs like that though. Granted, everyone has a way to control their sub, but I like to do it through our play."

She shivered, and he moved away again, stepping in front of her.

"Turn around, love," he said.

She tried not to pay attention to what pet name he called her, especially love. Nicola had a feeling he used it with all his subs. While it wasn't common in the United

States, it was in England. Making more of it would end in heartache.

She pushed that thought aside and turned.

"Take those delectable panties off, just leave them on the floor, then I want you on your knees on the bench. Hands on the mattress."

Nicola had to fight the urge to rip her own panties off. Instead, she took her time, bending over as she slipped the delicate fabric down her legs. She took her time straightening and he chuckled.

"I'll make you pay for that temptation."

She got into position, he walked over to the bed and picked up the flogger. He moved it to and fro, showing her he knew how to handle himself. What was she thinking? Of course he knew how to handle himself. He'd been a Dom for several years now, and she knew he had a reputation.

He slid the tassels of the flogger down her back and she waited.

"Spread your legs apart and keep your head up. You know the rules. No coming until I let you. And as always, use your safe word if I go too far."

It was the only warning she got before the flogger came down hard on her ass. He hit the exact same spot he had smacked earlier, and she knew it was no accident. Her flesh was already sensitive there, and the smack of the flogger heightened her arousal. He flogged her twice more in that spot before moving onto her right butt cheek. Again, and again, he brought the flogger down on her ass. She curled her fingers into the comforter as each slap increased her craving. The vibrations from the punishment left her pussy deliciously damp. Need crawled through her. Need to moan, need to come....need for him. More than once, she almost came from the flogging alone.

He stopped abruptly, then she felt his cool palm against her heated skin. The simple caress was almost tender, considering his actions just moments before.

"So gorgeous," he muttered, hunger deepening his voice. She felt his lips against her skin and she closed her eyes. The moan that escaped came from some place within her she didn't control.

He gave her cheek one last caress before he leaned over her. When he spoke, he whispered in her ear. "Always show me your pleasure, love. It lets me know what you like, what I can do to push those very tight buttons of yours."

He took her earlobe between his teeth and tugged. Then, he stepped away. Nicola heard the clunk of the flogger on the dresser. When he returned to the bed, he helped her situate herself on the bench once more, before grabbing the vibrator.

"Now, love, come closer to the edge and spread those legs. I want to see my pussy."

She wasn't too happy with the word *my* and opened her mouth to respond, but he slapped her sex.

It didn't hurt of course. Instead, her pussy lips contracted as she fought against the orgasm. Fuck.

"I didn't ask for your opinion. Just do what I say."

The authority in his voice was quiet, controlled, and that was more arousing than anything he could do to her physically. This wasn't her Jensen, the man she knew so well. This was Sir, the man of her dreams, the one that could make her orgasm with just a few words.

She spread her legs and he hummed. Those hums of his were as delicious as the physical things he was doing to her body.

"Incredibly wet. Your lips are dripping, love," he said as he slid his fingers over her. Then, he lifted his hand to his mouth. As he made eye contact, he tasted her on his fingers. Another hum.

"Just as I expected. Delicious."

His British accent seemed to deepen as it rolled over the syllables of the last word. He placed a hand on each of her thighs and leaned over and licked her sex. He teased her slowly, surely. After slipping her legs over his shoulders, he bent his head and devoured her. It was the only word she could use to describe what he did to her. Repeatedly, he slipped his tongue inside, then up and over her clit. Nicola fell back against the bed as she fought the orgasm that seemed to have her dangling on the edge. And at the point where she thought she couldn't fight it any longer and decided to deal with the consequences, he moved away from her.

"Nicola," he said.

She opened her eyes. Once again, he waited until her gaze met his. Then, without warning, he smacked her pussy again and left his hand there so she couldn't squeeze her legs together.

"I said don't come."

He slid his hand away to grab the vibrator. "You're wet enough that we don't need lube. At least I am assuming."

She nodded. He slid the vibrator into her pussy and turned it on. He didn't linger at the lower levels. Instead, he turned it up on high. As he pushed it to the hilt, he leaned down and kissed her. Just the softest of kisses at first, then he slid his tongue into her mouth. There she tasted herself, adding another layer to his seduction. He pulled back.

"Do you want to come?" he asked.

She opened her eyes. "Yes, sir."

"I'm just not sure."

He turned the vibrator up a notch as he thought about it.

She ground her teeth together as she fought against her need for release.

He pulled the vibrator away. "Not just yet. I'm not doing this to be mean, but I want to test you. I need to know your limits."

She said nothing, but took a deep breath trying to gather her control for the next challenge.

"Sit up, love." He waited for her to do so. "Pull down my boxers just so my cock is free."

Eager for this, she finished the task in a matter of just a few seconds.

"That's far enough," he said when she had exposed his cock and sac. "You may touch, but not too much."

She licked her lips as she wrapped her hand around him. She knew there would be hell to pay for it, but it was time to pay him back for leaving her this aroused. Slowly, she pumped him a couple times. He settled his hands on his hips and groaned.

"Take me in your mouth. I want to feel your tongue on my flesh."

Nicola had him in her mouth before he could finish the second sentence. She loved giving oral and she showed it to him. Over and over, he thrust into her mouth. She knew just how to position her throat for him, which brought about another groan.

"Bloody hell. I've been having so many fantasies about this, but none of those were this good."

That was all the encouragement she needed. She sped up her movements and soon he was in rhythm with her. Each time she rose to the top of his cock, she would swirl her tongue over his head. Nicola knew she was inching him closer to release and she wanted that. She wanted to feel him explode in her mouth and feel all the cum sliding down her throat.

Jensen had other plans.

"Enough of that, Nicola," he said, but he took his cock in his hand and lifted it. "Suck."

Nicola leaned forward to lick and suck his balls. Again, she pushed him, enjoying this part of the play too. He was keeping control of himself, but she knew that with each lick, he was getting closer.

Before she was really ready to stop, he was pulling away from her again. "Up on the bed, love. I want to see how that pussy of mine feels when I fuck you."

She really did like a man who was good at dirty talk. As she pulled down the comforter, then lay on the sheets, he rolled on a condom. He slipped over on top of her, then rose to his knees, grabbed her by the hips and entered her in one hard thrust.

"Bloody hell, that feels good."

He held them there for a long moment. Her sex pulsed around his cock. She closed her eyes and moaned. The sheer pleasure of being connected to him in this way almost overwhelmed her.

When he slowly pulled out of her, then drove back in, they both moaned together. Again and again, he pushed them further to the edge.

"Wrap your legs around me, love."

With each thrust, the connection between them seemed to grow. Instead of just the thrill of D/s play, this was something more. She wanted to fight against it, but she knew in her head that she couldn't, not any more. Fear rose up out of nowhere, and she did try to fight it then. She couldn't let go, not now. It would leave her vulnerable, more so than she had been in years.

She lost the battle before the war was even started. With him like this, she couldn't hide away, ignore the feelings she had been battling for months. They rushed forward taking control of everything: her heart, her mind, her soul. The arousal he had built was no longer just for sex, but something more. Something that pierced the shield she had erected years before. Her cheeks felt wet and she realized she was crying. She never cried during sex, but in one session, he brought it out in her.

He leaned down to kiss her as he continued to move within her. "Come, love. Come with me. Let me feel all those tiny little muscles on my cock."

Again, before he could finish telling her, she was already complying with his demands. Her orgasm hit her hard, pulling a scream from her so loud it surprised both of them. He chuckled, then groaned as a second orgasm hit her, her convulsions pulling him deeper inside of her. His movements became more erratic; hurried as if something else was driving him now. Only two more thrusts and he took his release, shouting her name as they both lost themselves to pleasure.

JENSEN WOKE A SHORT TIME LATER, Nicola in his arms, her body pressed against his and it felt so right. There was no other way to describe the way he felt right now. At that moment, he couldn't even fathom sleeping without her by his side. He traced her spine with his fingers. So strong, but delicate. That summed up Nicola to a T.

"I'm trying to sleep, buster," she said, humor lacing her voice. He smiled.

"I think we established you were going to call me Sir."

"Only during play."

He smacked her bottom, then rubbed the spot. "I had no idea what a great sub you would be."

She lifted up, balancing her weight on her hands. "Really? I excel at everything I do."

"Modesty."

She rolled her eyes, then dropped down on the mattress. He slipped his arm around her and pulled her close. She settled against his chest with a sigh. "When something is important, I try very hard at it."

"What I meant is that I would have pegged you for a Domme, not a sub."

She shrugged. "I wanted one place in my life where I didn't have to be in charge."

He absorbed the comment. "Your relationship with Oliver?"

"Yes?"

"You were the one in charge?"

"In the bedroom? Do you really want to talk about that?"

"Good God, no. I meant, your relationship was tangled up with your skating career. From everything I saw, you were the one in charge of those interviews."

She shifted, and he realized she did that so she could see his face. "You watched my interviews?"

"A few." All of them he could find, in fact, but he would never admit it. When Nicola had gone on vacation, he'd started his search for them. He told himself that it was for research, which had been a lie. Interviews over a decade old wouldn't tell him anything about Nicola. It was because he missed her, and now he could admit it to himself.

"What?" she asked.

"Nothing."

"You just had a look on your face."

He shrugged but said nothing. He was coming to the realization that this woman was more to him than simply the average sub. She was in his mind, his head. Fuck, as corny as it sounded, she was in his bloody soul. He was approaching forty and had never really been in love—well other than with heroin when he was still using. That had been his focus for so many years. He had been *in like* a few times, and definitely *in lust*, but he was beginning to worry that he was falling in love with Nicola.

"Jensen, really, you're freaking me out."

He shook his head. "I'm worn out. Seems I have this sub who likes to challenge me."

She gave him a blinding smile. "I told you I like to succeed."

"I need some rest before round two, so go to sleep."

As she settled her weight against him, he stared up at the ceiling. The few days they had left in Hawaii would never be enough. The idea of just walking away now left him slightly ill and frantic.

It struck him then that she was a bit like his addiction. He worried that she might not be there someday. Now that they had stepped over the line, he wasn't sure he could ever go back. One thing was for sure: he would do everything in his power to convince her to continue their affair.

chapter twelve

Nicola awoke slowly the next morning. It wasn't like her. Usually she woke up refreshed and ready to take on the day. When she moved, she groaned. Her muscles were sore. Like a hard workout on the ice sore. She opened her eyes and realized she wasn't in her room.

The memories from the night before washed over her. She turned her head and found the bed empty. Sitting up, she looked around the room. The first rays of sun crept into the room through the opened French doors.

"Well, that's a pretty sight," Jensen said.

She turned her head in the direction of his voice. He was shirtless, wearing those same silk blue PJ bottoms as the day before. His hair was mussed. She had seen it that way on long plane rides, but she had never seen him like this. The morning after made it even more intimate.

"Nicola?"

"Sorry." He walked toward the bed and she realized he had two cups of coffee. She took the one he offered her and took a sip. It was made up just the way she liked it. Her eyebrows rose.

"What?" he asked.

"It's made the way I like it and it doesn't suck."

"Marta's already here."

"Marta's here?" She closed her eyes. They had wanted to keep their relationship quiet, and this was not the way to do it.

"Don't worry. I brought your robe to the room and Marta is busy making a wonderful breakfast for both of us." He sat down on the bed. "I still have not heard a thank you from you."

"For what?"

"The coffee."

She smiled. "Thank you for having Marta make my cup."

Jensen frown. "I made your cup, woman."

"Really? You know how I like my coffee?"

"Yes. You like it to be the color of a camel, with two sugars."

He sounded so disgusted that she didn't believe him, she leaned forward and kissed him. "Sorry. Thank you."

"Four years of being in each other's pockets, I think I would know."

"I apologize."

He grumbled before taking a sip of his own coffee.

"I need to shower."

"Yes, and we have a teleconference this morning."

"What?"

"With the Johnsons. I was checking my email earlier—"

"How long have you been up? Why did you let me sleep so late?" She started to slip out of bed, but he set his hand on her thigh. Even through the sheets, she could feel his body heat.

"It isn't that late. It's just after six. They emailed me last night."

"When do they want to start?"

"They said eight, I asked them to push it back to ten."

She studied him for a second, as she sipped her coffee. "And why would you do that?"

"Because they have to understand that I'm not sitting around waiting for them."

"But we are in a way."

"Because we choose to. I knew you wanted to come over here to spend some time with Serenity, so I told Mother it was best we did it this way."

She blinked. "You did not. Your mother insisted. That's what you told me."

"I lied."

For a long moment, she couldn't think of what to say. They were there for the business dealings, that was true, but with today's technology, there was no reason for them to physically be there. They could have done this from England. It was true his mother liked the personal touch, but she had thought it a little odd they were in Hawaii.

"Are you telling me you came halfway across the world for no other reason than I could spend time with Serenity?"

Now, he didn't look so sure of himself. He shrugged and looked out the doorway that led to the balcony.

Dammit, why did he have to do that? She was already in danger of falling completely in love with the man, and he had to turn sweet?

Nicola leaned forward and brushed her lips against his cheek. He looked at her with his eyebrows raised.

"What was that for?"

"Until tonight," she said with a smile. She grabbed her robe, slipped it on, then rose out of bed. He tried to grab her hand as she tied the belt. "Nope. It's work time. I need a shower and to get ready for the day."

"Fine, be that way," he said, but she heard the humor in his voice. She opened the door and stuck her head out into the hallway to be sure no one was around, then slipped out into the hallway, closing the door behind her quietly. She hurried to her room, trying to get her mind wrapped around the idea of what had transpired the previous night. She turned on her shower, then waited for the water to heat up. She studied herself in the mirror. There was whisker burn on her breasts and she looked happy. Not just happy. Beyond happiness. She wasn't sure she had ever experienced a night with a Dom like she had last night. The only one who came close was Micah, and that was only because he was her first Dom.

That meant Serenity had been right. Sure, Nicola knew she had feelings for Jensen, but she didn't know the depths of them until last night. One could argue that it had more to do with their friendship, but she had been friends with some of the Doms she played with for three or more years. This didn't account for the way she felt when they made love a second time and she cried again. She never cried during sex, but she had twice in one night with Jensen.

The mirror was starting to fog, and she realized that she had been standing there for too long. Before she could step into the shower, her phone buzzed. She noticed it was Julienne. Damn, she didn't need this. Not right now when she was trying to figure out what last night had meant to her. But then again, there was a good chance she would never figure that out.

"Hey," she said answering the phone.

"Where have you been? I tried calling at what would

have been eight at night your time last night and you weren't answering."

I was letting your brother do all kinds of deliciously naughty things to me.

"Nowhere. Had a headache and went to bed early. What's up?"

"Nothing much, just wanted to make sure you hadn't killed Jensen yet.

"So, you haven't talked to him either?"

"I don't care *that* much. If he's gone, then Jakob and I can split the money."

She chuckled. "I was about to step into the shower."

"Oh, okay."

"We have a teleconference with the Johnson family this morning, afterwards I'll give you a ring, okay? I just want to get cleaned up since your brother just sprung this on me. No warning, just threw it out there."

"Brilliant. I'll talk to you later, ta."

She hung up before Nicola could respond. With a sigh she clicked off her phone and stepped into the shower. Time to get her head on straight so they could get to work.

AFTER A MASSIVE BREAKFAST and lots of coffee, Nicola's ability to think was back. She didn't know why they had wanted this meeting, but it was definitely a ploy of some sort. The Wulfs didn't do that many takeovers and, truthfully, she never had much to do with these kinds of proceedings. This was different, though. It wasn't as much as a takeover, but a helping hand. She knew the Johnson's had no reason to trust them, but as far as she knew, The Wulf family had never taken over a family business—ever. They tended to help with capital, with the agreement of the ability for a buyout. It was a win for both sides of the business.

Jensen had pulled a chair up beside him for the meeting. She sat down and tried to ignore the clean, masculine scent of him. He didn't use cologne, but he bathed in a sandalwood soap that she loved.

"Are you ready?" she asked.

Jensen answered, looking at her over the top of his reading glasses again. He really needed to quit doing that. It was rather silly how it turned her on so much, but it did. Why had she come up with a stupid rule about no play during work hours?

"Yes."

The computer played a tune, telling them that the other group was calling them. Jensen clicked to accept the call.

"Good morning," he said.

She recognized the group sitting there. All of them—minus the older son—were seated around a conference table. Robert sat at the head of the table.

"Good morning," Robert said.

He was the oldest, his hair stark white and years in the sun had weathered his skin. As the patriarch, he'd run the family business for all of his adult life. She knew the story of how he started from nothing, working to build massive wealth, which he was now in danger of losing.

To his right sat Michael, his son and Vice President. He only had a few stands of gray in his hair, but he looked to be a little shorter and a bit heavier than his father. While his father wore a Hawaiian shirt—typical on the islands even in business—Michael was dressed in a suit. On the opposite side of the table sat Lana and Sam. Lana was Michael's younger sister. She wore what looked to be a dress with massive pink plumeria. Her hair was a long waterfall of black, and while she was only one or two years younger than Michael, she looked much younger. Sam was dressed like his grandfather in a Hawaiian shirt. His dark black hair was cut short.

"So, do we have anything to discuss?" Jensen asked.

Robert's lips twitched. "That's one thing I like about you, Wulf. Always right to the point."

"My mother taught me there are times to be direct."

"Yes. Well, we are definitely interested and want to accept the offer."

"I feel there is a *but* in there."

"We have a few little things we want added to the contract."

"Okay. These have not been brought up before?"

He shook his head. "We want it in the contract that we keep the name of the resort."

"Of course, that goes without saying."

"And the buyout you offer?"

"You say in ten years we can buy back your half of the resort at market value."

"Yes?"

"We would like it at five years after the agreement. Then a clause to allow us to revisit every five years thereafter."

"I see no reason why that would be a problem."

While Jensen and Robert spoke, she watched the reaction of the other family members. Sam and Lana showed no outward reaction. If they disagreed with the contract, or the ideas Robert was putting forth, they weren't showing it. Michael was another matter. He was stoic, but his jaw kept flexing, telling Nicola that he was grinding his teeth. The others might not like the idea, but Michael seemed to be furious.

Robert and Jensen continued to chat about the contract, and then, Michael proved her right.

"I am raising my objection to this again," he said, interrupting his father mid-sentence.

From Lana and Sam's expressions, Michael had committed a huge faux pas. Apparently, interrupting Robert was not considered a good thing to do. From the look on Robert's face, he was not happy whatsoever.

"We voted, Michael. You even got hold of Aleka to get his vote, and he agreed. You lost four to one."

Michael slammed his fist on the conference table. "I have a right to run this company to fix the wrongs," he said, his voice raising louder with each word.

"Fix the wrongs? Michael, we talked about this," Lana said, glancing at the monitor. "The Wulfs know it, so I might as well say it. We need their money. Otherwise, we'll have to sell the resort to outsiders."

"Who the hell are the Wulfs?" he shouted, his face turning red.

"We are outsiders, that is true, but we do not want to own your resort outright. We want to help you."

"Why?" Michael said.

"My mother has her reasons, and she has not shared them with me. But I do know she researched your family. We are a family-run business, as you are. Your father has taken pains to ensure that all of you have a legacy. My mother admires that. She also doesn't like the idea of people coming in and taking over your business."

"That's it?" he said, his tone telling Nicola he didn't believe it.

"Our lawyers read over the contract, Dad," Sam said. "It's good. It will be good, and we'll be able to hire a lot of local workers for the hotel and the improvements. It will help the economy."

He shook his head, but Robert apparently had had enough.

"We voted, you lost." He turned toward the monitor. "If you can draw up the newest contracts, we will have our lawyers look them over. But, if nothing changes other than those things we talked about, I say you have yourself a deal."

"Brilliant. I'll contact my legal department about sending those over. Is Alfie around?"

Robert shook his head. "He said he was going to take a day or two and explore some of the other islands."

"Okay. Well, I'll have him take care of getting the contracts to you. Mother will definitely want to talk to you at some point, I'm sure."

"Until next time," Robert said, and the screen went black.

"That's a load off my mind," Jensen said.

"Hmm."

"What?"

"Michael made me a little nervous. He has a temper."

"He didn't get that from his father."

She chuckled. "That's true. At least everyone else—even the absent Aleka—agrees with the idea."

"Once we start working on the resort, he'll change his mind."

Before they could talk more, his phone vibrated on the desk. "Mother."

"Have fun," she said, gathering up her things.

He grabbed her hand. "Thank you."

"For what?"

"For your help with this."

"I barely did anything."

"I know that's not true. You did an extensive background check on the family, and I know that you greased the wheels a bit with local business owners."

"Just part of my job."

"And you are very good at your job."

"Thank you," she said. "Tell your mother. She'll be thrilled."

He smiled and released her hand. Then, as she left the room she heard him say, "Hello, Mother."

She closed the door and walked outside. It was a bit overcast and humid, telling her there was a good chance at thunderstorms later on in the day. Her phone buzzed, and she looked down to find that it was Jules.

"Hey."

"Hey, you didn't call me back."

"We just got done."

"Looking good?"

"They had a couple tweaks to the contracts, but it looks like other than that it is a done deal."

"Mother will be happy."

"Yes, Jensen's talking to her right now."

"What was that?"

"What?"

"The way you said Jensen's name was weird."

"It was not."

"Did he do something?"

Yeah, me.

"No. I was just a little unnerved by Michael."

"He's the VP and the son, right?"

"Yes. He was not in agreement. The others weren't happy, but they agreed they needed our help. He yelled and pounded his fist. I hope he isn't going to be a problem."

"Leave him to me. When I show up to handle the redesign, I'll charm him.'

Nicola didn't doubt it. All of the Wulf siblings were pretty good at charming, especially Americans. They heard that accent, along with their good looks, and all three of them could get anything they wanted.

"Is that what you called about earlier?"

"No. David is a bit worried about Gregor. He's making noises that he wants to reconcile."

"Really?"

"Yeah. If I thought it was because he loved me, I would do it in an instant."

"How do you know it isn't?"

"The stupid wanker told me. He said that I should be thinking of his political future."

"Good God."

"Right? I told him thinking of that still wouldn't give me an orgasm."

"You did not."

"I did. Wanker. He acted like I didn't even deserve romance."

"Every woman deserves romance."

"Right, so I told him to bugger off and hung up on him."

She sighed. "I'll make a few calls and make sure there isn't anything being shopped around."

"Thanks. I appreciate it. David is getting better, but he doesn't have your connections."

"He will someday."

"Right. Okay, I'm sure Mother will want to talk to me soon about the redesign, so I am going to start researching. Ta."

She disconnected without waiting for a response. Nicola clicked off her phone and sat down at the table. Last night and today had left her a bit frazzled. Mostly last night. Truthfully, though, she did not like Michael's reaction. He should be the one on board, but there seemed to be a split in the family. Things like that could lead to lawsuits, depending on how the business is run, but it could also lead to resentment. That is never a good thing in a family business.

With a sigh, she looked out past the backyard to the ocean behind it. The wind created choppy waters, but it felt good against her skin. So, she had things to worry about, but right now, Nicola decided she would think about all of that later and just enjoy the scenery for a while.

JENSEN WATCHED her through the kitchen window. She looked lost in thought, so he decided to ignore his need to be near her and just observe. Nicola had good instincts, so if she was worried about Michael, he needed to have him checked out. Jensen didn't think Michael would do anything to hurt the family. Michael was worried about the family and that the Wulf's were taking advantage of them. Only time would prove him wrong. He just needed to make sure that Michael didn't do anything to jeopardize the deal, namely offending the Wulfs. Going to the press and complaining about outsiders coming in to take over a locally-owned business could really hurt the deal. His mother would not stand for it.

He wanted more than anything to go out to the lanai and coax Nicola back to his room. They had only made love twice the night before, and he definitely knew it wasn't enough.

Would it ever be enough?

That thought slipped beneath his skin and made him itch. Even standing here, with Marta puttering around in the background, he was getting hard thinking about spanking Nicola again. She had responded so well. As soon as he realized he was thinking of doing just what he had been daydreaming about, he forced himself away from the window.

"Going to head back to the office if Nicola is looking for me. I have some lawyers to talk to."

"Of course," Marta said with a smile. He shoved his hands into his pockets, and after one last glance at Nicola enjoying the morning on the lanai, he turned and headed back to his office. The sooner he was finished with work, the sooner he could call it the end of the work day.

And then he could have Nicola all to himself once again.

chapter thirteen

Three days later, Nicola was having lunch with Jeff and Ben at a popular chain restaurant in the Aloha Tower Marketplace. It had gorgeous views of the water, and they, luckily, were seated outside. It provided a wonderfully cooling breeze.

Jeff was about the same age as she was, only a few months older. His blond hair was still as short as it had been during their skating days, but he had put on a few pounds. During everything, he could always make her laugh, and when everyone else tuned their backs on her, he had stood by her. He was the one friend from her skating days that she knew she could count on. Ben, his husband and business partner, was shorter, with dark hair and a lean, wiry body that spoke of his marathon training. If Jeff was loud and amusing, Ben was a calming influence.

Within moments of sitting down, she knew something was up. She'd had a bit of a scuffle with Jensen before leaving, because he hadn't wanted her to go. In fact, he tried to order her not to go, she just laughed and walked out the door. He hadn't been serious, it worried her anyway. He tended to get into trouble when he was left at loose ends, she couldn't help it though. She had always drawn a definitive line between work and her personal time. Unfortunately, that was getting a little blurry thanks to their new connection.

"I should have never forgiven you after you left me out in the cold," Jeff said.

"In the cold?" she asked with a laugh. "What the bloody hell are you talking about?"

Jeff shook his head. "There you go again."

"What?"

He waited a second, then he offered her an evil grin. "Sounding like a Brit."

"Bite your tongue, Jeffy. And how did I leave you in the cold?"

"When you were hired by Jensen Wulf. I could have turned him."

Ben shook his head and smiled, saying nothing.

"Technically, his mother hired me first as his sober companion. Also, you would have never turned him. He has no interest whatsoever in men."

"I disagree."

"You would be wrong, but then that wouldn't be the first time."

He opened his mouth to argue with her, but his husband changed the subject.

"One thing I have always been interested in is the history of the Wulf family," Ben said.

"How so?" she asked.

Ben waited as their waiter returned to the table with their entrees.

"I mean, it doesn't sound very English or proper."

She chuckled. "Well, they aren't *that* English. The truth is, their proper last name was Wulfgang. They changed it after World War I."

"Hmm, that is really interesting."

"Right? A large number of people with even the hint of German in their name changed it, including the Windsors. Of course, the Wulfs no longer lay claim to their aristocratic name."

"Very interesting."

"I find them all endlessly fascinating," Jeff said.

She had just taken a bite of her fish when she noticed a movement out of the side of her eye. The last few years had taught her to be wary of such things. Keeping all of the Wulf siblings out of the press was important. She looked over and saw nothing. Positive she had made a mistake, she concentrated on eating.

"You would," she said after swallowing. "It isn't as fun as it looks in the press."

"And you started working for the Bad Boy Billionaire when he stopped being a bad boy."

"Hmm," was all she said to that. She couldn't tell either Ben or Jeff about her and Jensen. Both of them were horrible gossips. They wouldn't purposely leak the information, but they couldn't be trusted to keep their mouths shut.

Again, the feeling of eyes on her had her looking around. Then she saw him. Hiding behind some greenery. It was the only explanation for it. Jensen Wulf, CEO of Wulf Industries and blood-related to the Windsor family, was hiding behind a palm plant spying on her. She blinked trying to see if he would disappear.

She dabbed her mouth, then said, "Excuse me for a moment."

Both of the men nodded and paid little attention to her. As she rose and started in his direction, she saw panic move over his expression. She grabbed him by the wrist and never stopped her forward progression toward the bathroom. She stopped in the alcove that lead there.

"What the hell are you doing here?"

"I just happened—"

"Don't even try that."

He sighed and pulled off his sunglasses. "I was worried."

"About what?"

"About this meeting."

"It isn't a meeting. It's lunch with an old friend and his husband. You can't be jealous. They're gay."

"It's not that."

"What?"

He looked past her, but she could tell he wasn't focusing on anything in particular. Nicola knew he did this for one of two reasons. Either he was avoiding the subject, or he was coming up with an excuse that was closer to a lie than to the truth.

"I was afraid they were trying to steal you away from me."

She blinked. "Steal me?"

"Yes. I thought they might want you to be the PA for his production company."

"And that's the only reason?"

Still without looking at her, he nodded. She had no reason to think he wasn't telling the truth.

"Well, you don't need to worry about that. I wouldn't work for either one of them because they would drive me crazy. Also, they spent half an hour telling me that they are going to have another reality show. Can you imagine me on a reality show? That would end badly for everyone involved."

His mouth curved, and his shoulders relaxed a bit.

Finally, his gaze met hers. "You do not do well in those situations."

"So, go away. You can meet the guys another time, but right now is *my* time."

"For a sub, you're a bossy bit of goods."

She smiled. "Not a sub right now. I'll be home in a bit."

When she turned away, he grabbed her hand and tugged her back. With the barest of touches, he brushed his mouth over hers. It was the first time he had done anything like this in public. They had agreed not to, but there was a part of her, a big part of her, that craved his touch, no matter where they were. And right now, they weren't employer and employee. They were just Jensen and Nicola. She shivered, leaning into the kiss, enjoying the way his lips moved over hers.

He pulled back before she was ready. She opened her eyes and found him shaking his head at her. When he spoke, his voice wasn't that steady.

"You are one dangerous woman, Nicola McCann."

Then he was walking away from her. She couldn't go right back to the table. The guys would know something was up. Instead, she went into the bathroom and splashed some water on her face. After grabbing a few paper towels, she dried off her face and caught a glimpse of herself in the mirror. Maybe it was her imagination, but she looked different. Happy. Had she not been happy before? She had but there had been some element missing in her life. Dammit, she didn't need this, didn't need the heartbreak that was definitely going to follow. They weren't made for each other.

Although, when they were together in his bedroom, it felt perfect.

She shook her head. *Get your head out of your ass, Nicola*, she thought to herself. This was not forever. It was for right now.

She straightened her shoulders and headed back out into the restaurant. When she sat down, both men looked at her as if she had grown a horn in her forehead.

"What?"

"We have something to talk to you about, and we don't want you to say no right away," Ben said.

Oh, God, they were going to ask her to work for them. Damn Jensen for being right. She would never admit it to him.

"Guys, I love you, you know that. But working for you is just not a good thing."

Jeff threw his head back and laughed so loud it drew attention. Ben smiled at her.

"Jeffy, cut it out."

"Oh, I struck a nerve," Jeff said. "That's not what we want to talk about. Our PA has to work on the show, in front of the camera, and while you make a pretty picture, you have no patience these days. No. We have something much more serious to ask you. And, like Ben said, don't answer us right now."

She looked from one man to the other. "Okay, lay it on me."

WHEN JENSEN LEFT THE RESTAURANT, he ordered John to just drive to H-3. He didn't realize it at the time, but he was headed to Serenity's home. Going home would leave him at loose ends and that was never a good thing for an addict. Nicola didn't keep any liquor in the house when they were on the island. She would buy wine specifically for a meal if they were hosting, but she knew it was important for him not to be tempted.

Still, he wasn't in the mood to be there without her. He was relieved when they pulled into the parking area where Serenity and her men lived. There were two houses on the property. Serenity had lived in one until she moved in with her men. The smaller house was now just for her studio for her photography business. He slipped out of the car and started toward the bigger of the two houses.

"Hey, Jensen," Serenity called out from the porch of her studio. "Guys aren't home today. They had a job on Maui."

"Oh."

"Nicola isn't here either."

"I know."

She said nothing as she sipped from a coffee mug. "Come on in. I'm just playing with some pics I took. I'll make you real coffee."

He nodded and followed her into her house.

"What do you mean real coffee?"

She frowned. "The guys won't let me have caffeine. Someone has been doing research and found out that it's really bad for the fetus."

"Ah," he said wandering over to her computer. Then he saw the pics she was working on. It was from his house, by the pool.

Nicola.

She was wearing that stupidly big straw hat she loved. A pair of glasses hid her eyes, but the smile was genuine. In fact, she looked to be laughing. He loved that sound, the way it always seemed to dance through the air and make the atmosphere so much better.

"She's an easy subject," Serenity said.

He didn't take his gaze from the screen. "Yeah. And the woman does love to laugh. Usually at my expense."

"Oh."

There was something in her tone that pulled his attention away from the picture.

"What?"

She shook her head. "Nothing."

"No, you said oh, so that means something."

She sighed. "You're in love with her."

Not a question, but a statement. "You know of our arrangement?"

She nodded. "I was probably the only person she told."

"Of course you were. That woman holds onto secrets. Especially when talking about her past."

"You're talking about Oliver?"

He nodded.

The kettle whistled, and she hurried over to it. After filling a French press with coffee, she poured in the water. Then she grabbed him a mug.

"I can't tell you anything, because it's her story to tell. But, I think you should ask her about it."

He wanted to, but he was also worried she would refuse to tell him. She was habitually secretive about that part of her life. If he asked now, and she said no, it would be like she was trying to hide something from him. As if he were just another man in a long line of men.

"You take your coffee black, right?" she asked.

"Yes."

She handed him the mug. "She'd tell you."

"She hasn't in the past."

"It's different now."

He shrugged as he sipped his coffee.

"Also, the fact that she is involved with you now, that makes a big difference."

"How so?" he asked.

She sat down at the kitchen table and motioned toward the other seat. He sat and waited.

"Nicola tries to keep men at arm's length. She might spend more than one night with them over a course of years—"

"Don't need to know that."

She smiled. "So cute that you're jealous. Those men, they weren't important. Not to her."

"You talk in riddles."

Instead of taking offense, she laughed. He had spent time with Serenity through the years, but never one on one. As Nicola said, it was really hard to stay mad at her. When he had first met her, Jensen had expected the former child star to be more...well, Hollywood. Instead, she was warm and open, without the artifice so many people in show business never seem to shake.

"What I mean is that her time with each man was short. She might hook up again with them, but she never truly builds anything substantial past the sex with them."

"That's a good thing?" he asked, irritated that Nicola's sex life sounded close to what he usually insisted on.

"And I can see it there. You know that she insists on it too just like you. But this is different, for both of you. You have never been this close to one of your subs, have you?"

He shook his head.

"She has also never been particularly close to any of her Dom's. Friendly, yes, but she rarely has experiences outside of the bedroom. Well, I mean, except for Micah."

He blinked. "Come again?"

"I said Micah. He was her first Dom, so that makes sense."

Serenity's tone told him that she thought Nicola had told him. Bloody hell. Neither of them had told him. Jensen had known there was something more than just friendship between them. Her first fucking Dom, and she was still friends with him. Well, not for much longer.

Dammit, he couldn't do that. She'd get huffy and kick him to the curb, and he wasn't ready for that. Would he ever be ready for that? Probably not.

Jesus hell, he was a mess.

"Jensen, is something wrong?"

"No, sorry. So, you were saying?"

"You both have never had a real relationship outside of the bedroom. You two know each other now, better than some spouses probably. It's going to be harder to walk away."

"I never said I wanted to walk away."

She nodded. "Good. Because I think you both could be happy if the relationship continued."

"It is my intention, but I knew I had to agree to some kind of end date. Nicola wasn't going to let it go on forever."

"Yeah, Nicola is big on plans." They shared a smile. "What are you doing for her birthday tomorrow?"

He said nothing.

"Please tell me you didn't forget about it."

"You just informed me I was in love with her. How would I have forgotten?"

"Good."

"I wondered if you could do something to help."

She gave him the blinding smile that had made her a child superstar.

"Anything."

NICOLA WALKED through the Aloha Tower Marketplace, her mind still whirling with what the guys had asked her. They dropped it in her lap and then said they had to run. Jeff hadn't changed since their years on the ice. He always threw out grenades and then ran for cover. At least they had paid for her lunch.

"Nicola?" she heard someone call out.

She turned and saw Alfie jogging toward her. He was the same age as Jensen but looked older. That said a lot because Jensen had been a user for a few years, while Alfie apparently had been into clean living. He wasn't as fit as Jensen, or as tall, but she knew women liked him. He always seemed to have one by his side at every function.

"Alfie. I didn't know you were on the island."

He gave her a lopsided smile she was sure worked on most women. It had always left her cold. "Not much to do while the Johnson family squabbles about the negotiations. Jensen told me to take some time to enjoy the islands. Is he around?"

She shook her head. "I was just having lunch with friends."

"Oh, I was going to ask you if you wanted to grab a bite."

Had he stepped closer? She wasn't sure, but she always felt off balance with him. Alfie was harmless, yet he always struck her as a user. If he thought she could do something for him, Nicola was sure he would be even nicer to her. That told her he wasn't a good study of human behavior. She never hid the fact of how she felt about users.

"So, how about dinner?"

She shook her head and tried to give him a sympathetic smile. "Sorry, I can't."

"Jensen can't have you working at night."

"Of course not. Besides, I had the day off. I already have plans."

She hoped that would be enough to discourage him. He had never shown much interest in her throughout the years. Still, she always thought he saw her as some kind of glorified secretary. Their last exchange had been him ordering her to get him coffee, and her ignoring him. Which begged the question, why the interest now?

"Shame. Maybe later this week? That is if the Johnson family doesn't call us back to Maui to discuss the deal again."

"Maybe. Why not text me and we'll try and set something up?"

He smiled, but it didn't reach his eyes. Instead, it chilled her blood. "Sounds like a great idea. Thanks, Nicola."

At that point, he did something completely out of character for him. He leaned in for a kiss, but she turned her head and took it on her cheek. When he pulled back, she thought she saw a flash of anger, but it vanished so quickly, she was sure she was mistaken.

"Talk to you soon," she said, doing her best to move away from him.

"You can count on it."

She said nothing else as she walked away from him. As she did, her phone buzzed. She saw Serenity's face on the screen and clicked it on to answer.

"Hey, you. What's up?" she asked.

"Nothing much, but I just had a strange visitor."

"That makes two of us," she said.

"You'll never guess who just left."

"Bruno Mars."

"Why would you pick him?"

"He's from Hawaii."

"Good Lord. No. Jensen."

She stopped walking, and the woman behind her ran right into her. Nicola almost fell over from the hit and the rude woman, who had to be a tourist from the sunburn and the attitude, sniffed in her direction. Nicola ignored her.

"What?"

"Yes, your boss and lover Jensen Wulf showed up here."

She blinked. "He just showed up?"

"Yes."

She massaged her temple. "He was here too."

"What do you mean?"

"When I was having lunch with Jeff and Ben, he was in the restaurant spying on me."

"What? Oh. My. Gawd. This gets more and more interesting. What happened?"

"I sent him away."

"That was all?"

"No. He kissed me, told me I was dangerous, then he left."

"Hmm."

"What did he want with you?" she asked as she started walking again.

"I'm not really sure. I thought he might be looking for the guys, but they're on Maui for a few days. I showed him some of my recent pics I was working on and we chatted. I think he was killing time until his lady love made it back to him."

"Stop that."

"You might not realize this, but that man has it *bad* for you."

Nicola handed the valet her ticket and waited. "He does not."

"Does too."

"You have no proof of that."

Serenity tsked. "He was spying on you in the restaurant, then he came here to kill time until you got home. Darling, that man is crazy about you. Did he say why he was spying on you?"

"He said he was worried that Ben and Jeff were going to hire me away from him."

"I call bull. That man just didn't know what to do without you around."

"My turn to call bull."

"Sure, sure. Either way, he left a few minutes ago, so I wanted to give you warning."

"Thanks. I'll call you later."

"Sure thing," she said. "Love you."

"Love you," she said, then clicked off her phone.

All worries of the conversation with Jeff and Ben, along with the weird encounter with Alfie, dissolved. They had nothing to do the rest of the day, and Jensen would be home soon. Anticipation and happiness danced through her blood. This would definitely call for a little play during the day.

chapter fourteen

The moment he arrived home, Jensen sent John off for the night. He definitely needed some alone time with Nicola. He slipped into the house and barely made a sound. It was almost silent, except for the murmur of a voice. He followed the sound out to the lanai.

"*Ma*ma, I don't know why they asked me, but I can assure you I said no."

Then she was silent.

"Who knows with Jeff?" she asked.

He must have moved because she looked over at him and smiled.

"It's getting late, so I'll talk to you tomorrow about this. Goodnight, *Ma*ma. Yes, I know it isn't night here, but it is there."

Then she hung up.

"I see you made it home safely," she said.

"Yes, hard not to with John at the helm."

"Hmm."

"So, what did they want?"

"What?"

"You said they asked you something. I heard you say it to your mother."

She shifted in her seat. "I don't want you to lose your temper over this."

"I knew it," he said, anger coursing through his blood. "You will call them right now and tell them you are not on the market. You work for me. You're mine."

"Excuse me?"

"I will not allow it."

"First of all, I didn't ask. Second of all, they did not want me working for them. They want me to be a surrogate."

He frowned and settled his hands on his hips. "A surrogate? For what?"

She rolled her eyes. "For them. They want to have a baby."

For a brief moment, his brain ceased to work. The image of Nicola's belly swollen with his child flashed through his thoughts. He couldn't shake it loose.

"Why are you staring at me like that?"

He shook his head but not the picture of a pregnant Nicola. "No reason."

The image still wouldn't get out of his head. He had never thought to have children. It wasn't something he yearned for—until now. He wanted them, and he wanted them with Nicola.

"That's what the guys wanted. They weren't interested in stealing me away from you."

"But they are." The idea that another man would have a child with her was unacceptable. Even through in vitro he would not stand for it.

"What?"

"You're going to be my PA while pregnant with their child? I don't think so."

Nicola's eyes narrowed as her spine straightened. In the four years he had known her, Jensen had learned that was not a look you wanted from Nicola. It usually ended with someone on the floor in a fetal position.

"First, I wasn't thinking about it. I told them I would because they wouldn't take no for an answer today. My plan was to let them down gently."

"Oh. Good."

"Although, if I decided to do it, I would do whatever the hell I wanted. There is nothing in my contract about having children. If there had been, I wouldn't have signed it."

She stood and walked past him. He knew he had made another faux pas when talking about pregnancies. It wasn't something he was accustomed to. Not with anyone, well, maybe except Nicola. He always seemed to make mistakes with her. Of course, she could be just the only person who pointed them out.

And that made him love her even more.

He grabbed her hand before she could escape. She stopped.

"I'm not in the mood now, Jensen."

He heard the irritation in her voice, but there was something else. Something that sounded a lot like hurt. It was the last thing he had wanted. But, just like their first morning after her dinner with Serenity, Jensen had said something that hurt her. Nicola wasn't a woman who was overly sensitive.

"Jensen, just let me go be mad."

"I'm okay with that. Except you aren't just mad. I'm sorry I hurt you."

She sighed, and her shoulders slumped. "You didn't hurt me. I'm made of strong stock, as my father likes to say."

"You are probably the strongest woman I know. It's not

that. I seemed to have touched a nerve and I didn't mean to."

She still wouldn't look at him, so he tugged her closer and slipped his arms around her. And there it was. That feeling of completeness. He knew that first night it was different, and each night the connection had grown stronger.

"I didn't mean anything by it. No, that's wrong," he said. She lifted her head and smacked him in the chin.

"What do you mean?"

"I panicked. The idea that they could steal you away with a job or a baby left me somewhat out of sorts."

She studied him, her expression guarded. "You panicked? Bollocks."

He smiled at her wordage. "True story. I know that you want a family someday."

"It wasn't something I was thinking about until lately."

Was it because of their relationship or because Serenity was pregnant? He hoped it had more to do with them, but he wasn't confident enough to ask her, not yet.

He bent his head and brushed his mouth over hers. Just that little touch spurred the already insatiable hunger he had for her. He didn't think it would ever change. At one time, he would have freaked out over the obsession he had for her.

Slipping his hands up her body, he cupped her face, deepening the kiss. Her tongue tangled against his, sending another electric shock of need buzzing through his body. He wanted her. That was nothing new. But he was damned close to stripping her down and taking her. Seeing that they were in the backyard and there were tons of tourists and locals out, that was probably a bad idea.

He forced himself to end the kiss, then stepped back, grabbing her hand and leading her to the stairs. He had never, in fact, had a regular submissive. There were friends he played with, but he'd never wanted one woman night after night. This was their fourth night together, and Jensen didn't think he would ever get enough of her.

He led her to his room. He wanted to call it their room, but even in his mind, he worried what she would think. She had slept with him ever since that first night together.

After entering the room, he let go of her hand and headed to the overstuffed chair sitting in the corner. He settled into it and watched her. There were subs who would play the part. They tended to like to please a Dom right off. Nicola was not one of those, and he thanked his maker for that small favor. She loved to be Dominated, definitely, but she made a Dom earn it. Or at least that is the way she was with him.

"Come over here, Nicola," he said.

She stepped over to him but not close enough. He motioned with his finger to get closer. Frowning, she did so.

"Now, love, it's time for you to strip."

She hesitated, but finally lifted her hands. Carefully, she pushed her hair over one shoulder, then she turned.

"I need help with the zipper."

Jensen hesitated, knowing that any touching by him and he might just lose his control. After a long moment, he finally shifted to the edge of the chair and undid her zipper. He didn't hurry, instead he took his time, allowing his fingers to tease her flesh. The pink fabric gave way to reveal a pink bra and yet another thong. The woman had a penchant for naughty lingerie, especially thongs.

When he finally had the dress unzipped, she let it fall to the floor at her feet. But, Nicola knew just how to get to him. She stepped out of the dress, then bent over, giving him a wonderful view of her world-class ass. He knew she still worked out, and she skated whenever she got the chance and it showed.

He leaned back in the chair just as she peeked back at him. The woman was a minx and truly the wickedest sub he had ever had.

He raised his eyebrows and waited for her to straighten. She sniffed, apparently not getting the reaction she wanted. His cock throbbed, but there was no way he was going to let her know about that. Instead, he kept his gaze steady.

"You'll pay for that later."

"You didn't say how to take off my clothes, Sir."

He couldn't fight the spiraling of heat that shot through his blood. Jensen got a thrill every time she used the word Sir when they were playing. It was the dichotomy of the woman he knew during the day, and the one he was getting to know at night in his bed.

"True, but from now on, know that I'm not going to put up with that."

She frowned, and it turned him on even more. He was sick. Everything she did seemed to give him a hard-on. Reaching behind her, she was about to undo her bra, when he stopped her.

"No, not yet. Come here."

She stepped closer. "Not close enough." He continued to crook his finger until she was standing between his legs.

"You do have the most delicious taste in lingerie." He lifted his hand to skim the flesh that rose above the lace of her bra. She shivered at the contact and he smiled. "Go ahead," he said. Take it off.

He waited as she reached behind her and unhooked the bra. She let it slide down her arms, but again, very slowly.

"Tsk, tsk," he said, taking the lace confection from her

and placing it on the arm of his chair. "But then, I have a reward for now."

He sat up straighter to take one nipple into his mouth as he pinched and teased the other. She moaned as he moved his mouth to the other nipple to give it the same treatment. Sliding his hands down, he cupped her ass, thanking God again for her taste in panties. The woman definitely knew how to focus on her assets.

As he started to lose his grip on his control, he grazed her nipple once more with his teeth, then pulled back.

It took him a second or two to gain his wits. He didn't look up at her, but he could feel her gaze on him. Right at this moment, if he wasn't prepared, he would forget the rules.

"Now, the panties."

He watched her nimble fingers slip beneath the fabric and slip the panties off her legs. It took a while because she had long legs, but he knew she was teasing him again. He wanted to smile, because he knew what she wanted, what she needed. If there was a woman made for spankings it was Nicola. He had never had a sub who enjoyed them so much.

She held her panties out to the side and dropped them.

"You like testing limits."

"Me?" she asked, her tone teasing. She knew just how to taunt him to get a rise out of him.

He motioned her away with his hand and he stood.

"Now, undress me, but, nothing else. No touching other than taking my clothes off."

She started with his shirt, pulling it out of his pants, then unbuttoning it. While she was occupied with that, he skimmed his hands over her shoulders, then down her sides. She giggled.

"I thought there was no touching, Sir."

"For you. I get to do whatever I want."

"I have a request, Sir."

"So nice now. What is your request."

"Not my sides. I'm very ticklish and it really ruins the mood for me."

He slid a finger beneath her chin and gently urged her to look up at him.

"Thank you for asking so nicely, and I will refrain. I didn't know you were ticklish."

She smiled. "Thank you, Sir."

"You're welcome. Now, continue on."

He removed his hand to let her look down to complete her task. She finished with his shirt, then pushed it down his arms and off. She reached for his pants, but he stopped her.

"No. On your knees, love."

She said nothing, but he saw the quick smile before it disappeared. She did as he ordered. When she reached for his pants, she slipped her fingers beneath the waistband just far enough to tease his cock.

"Nicola," he said.

She said nothing but unbuttoned, then unzipped his pants. As she slid the zipper down, she let her finger glide over his shaft. The woman might like being a submissive, but once again, she was testing his limits. Some Doms might not like it, but he loved it. He loved when a sub had enough backbone to challenge him. Nicola had proven over the last few nights that she had it in spades.

"That's enough. Take them off."

She did and reached for his boxers. She eased them off, teasing him just a little more. He would have reprimanded her, but he noticed that her fingers shook, telling him that she was just as affected by their play as he was.

"Now, normally I would spank you for what you pulled

just a few minutes ago. But, since I know you like that, I'm going to have you do something else." Jensen looked down at his cock. "Now that you caused this situation, I think you need to give me a little pleasure."

He took hold of his cock "Suck, love."

Nicola didn't hesitate. Opening her mouth, she took him in. He closed his eyes as the damp heat of her mouth surrounded his shaft. She slid her tongue over and around his cock, as she lifted her hand to massage his sac. Good God, the woman was a devil with that tongue. She pulled back then slid him back into her mouth. Slowly at first, then she moved her hand from his sac to his shaft, adding to the pleasure.

He opened his eyes and looked down as her head bobbed back and forth.

"Nicola, look at me."

She did but she didn't stop what she was doing. Bloody fucking hell. He almost came then and there when her gaze caught his. It was one of the most sensual things he had ever had done to him. It wasn't as insanely depraved as some of his sexual escapades, but it was that connection he had felt since that first night. She was everything he ever wanted in a woman—and more.

"Enough," he said gently urging her away, and leading her to the bed. He grabbed a condom and set it on the bedside table, then followed her onto the mattress. He wanted nothing more than to sink into her warmth and lose himself, but he had to make sure she was there with him.

He slipped between her legs, kissing his way all the way to her pussy. She was dripping wet, the scent of her arousal filling his senses. After kissing her stomach right above her sex, he took a taste. As it had been that first night, he savored her arousal as it danced over his taste buds. After one long lick, he slipped inside of her pussy lips, once, twice…

She started to squirm so he lifted his head and smacked her pussy. Her sharp intake of breath caught his attention.

"No coming until I tell you."

She frowned down at him, but she said, "Yes."

He smacked her again, and she shuddered.

"Yes, what?" he demanded.

"Yes, Sir," she said from behind clenched teeth. He didn't know if she was irritated or just turned on so much she was trying to control herself. Jensen would lay odds on the latter.

He bent his head and kept eye contact with her, he slipped his tongue over her clit before pulling it into his mouth. Her eyes slid closed and she arched of the bed.

"Oh, God."

"Nope," he said licking his lips. "Just Jensen or, in this case, Sir."

Nicola laughed but it ended on a moan. He wanted to play more, to push her to the edge, but Jensen knew he was rapidly losing control.

He grabbed the condom, opening the wrapper and then sliding it on. He slipped up her body, then kissed her, enjoying the way she hummed against his mouth. With quick moves, he rolled them over the bed. She sat up on top of him.

"Take me in, love."

She rose up taking hold of his cock, and slowly descended. Nicola kept eye contact the entire time. It seemed to take forever before he was fully seated inside of her. Then she started to move.

Nicola was a woman who knew just how to ride him. Each time she slid down on him, her inner muscles squeezed his shaft. At first, she was slow, but soon, her movements sped up. As he felt his orgasm approaching, he knew he didn't want to be alone. He slipped his fingers over her clit, teasing her into an orgasm.

"Come, Nicola. Let me watch you."

That was all she needed. She exploded, her body rocking with her orgasm, her muscles pulling him deeper into her core. He could hold back no longer. Grabbing hold of her hips, he thrust up into her, his own release taking over. After long moments, she collapsed on top of him.

He ran his hand down her spine, enjoying the feel of her against him, the way she fit right there. He cupped her ass.

"Hmm," she said. "Thank you, Sir."

"You are most welcome, love."

"May I make another request?"

He could tell by her tone she was apprehensive about it.

"Yes."

"Please don't call me love. Can you call me Nicola?"

"Why don't you want me to call you love?" Women. He would never understand them, especially this one.

"I just don't want to be called what you call other women you have had in your bed. I know this is temporary, but I really don't want to be lumped in with those women."

It was then that it hit him. She had no idea how their relationship was affecting him. He debated for about a second or two until he finally decided to tell her the truth.

"Nicola, look at me."

It took her a moment before she raised her head up.

"I swear that I have never called a sub *love* before. I promise."

"You're being truthful with me?"

He nodded.

Her expression lightened, and his damned heart almost melted right there. This woman had him by the bollocks and she had no idea. Even after what he told her, he knew that Nicola was his idea of the perfect sub.

She leaned up for a kiss. "Thank you, Jensen,"

Then she rested her head against his chest. In a matter of a few minutes her even breathing told him that she was asleep. He could lay awake worrying about their relationship, but he couldn't keep his eyes open. In moments, he felt himself falling asleep, promising to talk to her about their issues.

chapter fifteen

Nicola's phone buzzed just before six the next morning. She grabbed it and saw a pic of her mother on the screen. She glanced behind her to see if it woke Jensen, but he was already up and out of bed. Since that first night, that had been his routine each morning. It was odd for her.

She clicked her phone on.

"Happy Birthday," her parents said together.

"Thank you."

"You didn't answer the first time we called on the Face-Time," her mother said.

She smiled. "Sorry. I just woke up."

"That's late for you." As much as her mother and she had traveled for her skating career, her father hadn't done that much. Being in a different time zone was completely foreign to him.

"It is just before six, Dad."

"Ah. So, do you have the day off?" her father asked.

"I'm not sure. Jensen said we had something to do, but

he didn't really say what it was. Our work is just about wrapped up here."

"Are you going to have time to pop in? We haven't seen you in a long time," her mother said.

Nicola rolled her eyes. She had just seen them less than a month ago, but she did understand. She was their only child.

"I don't think so, but maybe next month? We don't have much on the schedule, and I would love to just hang out with you two for a little bit."

"That sounds fine," her father said. "Are you making Jensen take you out?"

She smiled. "No, not this year. Serenity has invited us over for dinner."

"That will be nice. Time with friends is important," her mother said. "We just wanted to call and wish you happy birthday. You should get some flowers from us today."

"Thank you."

"Happy Birthday," her mother said.

"Thank you. Love you two."

"Love you, little girl," her father said. Then he hung up. Before she could get her thoughts together, the door opened. Jensen was there, dressed in a pair of shorts and a Hawaiian shirt. But not an outlandish Magnum PI kind of shirt. It was red, with just one palm tree embroidered on it.

"Good morning, birthday girl. How are you feeling?" He leaned over her and gave her a loud smacking kiss.

She blinked, unused to this behavior. It wasn't that they didn't kiss, but...it was more intimate as if they were long time lovers.

"I'm fine. My folks just called. They asked when I was going to be able to come visit them."

He chuckled. "They are constantly asking you that. We

could stop on the way back. We have absolutely nothing pressing."

"You don't mind?" she asked.

He sat down beside her. "No. You know I like your parents, and I want to go to that Mexican all-you-can-eat restaurant."

Of course he did. Last time they were there, he ate so much food, she was surprised they didn't have to roll him out of the place.

"Well, I will tell them after we close the deal here. I want to make sure everything is in order."

He gave her another of those lopsided smiles that made her heart skip a beat. It was corny to think that, but there was no other way to describe the way her heart seemed to stop for just a second every time it happened.

"Sounds good. Now, time to get out of bed and into the shower. I have plans for you today."

"I thought we were just going to Serenity's tonight. I was promised shrimp truck shrimp."

"Yes, but I have stuff for us to do today."

She sighed. "I thought about just laying by the pool all day."

"While I would not mind seeing you in a bikini again, I have something very special for you this afternoon. Knowing my family, the calls will start soon, so I thought to get you up and out of bed early."

She frowned.

"Oh, don't do that. It's your birthday and you should be happy. Marta is making you one of your favorite breakfasts, and —"

"What?"

"Take a shower and you will see. Lots of surprises today. It isn't every day that a girl has a birthday and is in Hawaii."

"Fine." Then what he said hit her. "Marta's here? Good Lord."

"Oh, just let it go. If she doesn't already know something is going on, she is never going to know. Go take a shower."

She slipped out of bed and he whistled. "You do look beautiful in the morning, Ms. McCann. Of course, you're pretty much beautiful all the time."

He stood and slipped his arm around her waist and pulled her closer. He kissed her, his tongue slipping between her lips for just a second. He ended the kiss long before she was ready for him to stop.

"Now, love, go take a shower. I'll get you something to wear."

She gave him a suspicious eye. "I can get my own clothes."

He sighed. "Just go take a shower, woman. Truthfully, if we were staying longer, I would have you move your clothes in here."

Then, he left her in the room staring after him. The man was in the oddest of moods.

Deciding not to worry about those issues at the moment, she took a quick shower, and when she came out into his bedroom, she found a purple dress with large pink flowers on it. Beside it was a pink bra and the matching thong. She stepped closer and realized that Jensen must have bought the dress for her. It was just the kind of dress she liked to wear when they were some place tropical, and it was in a deep, rich amethyst, a color she liked to wear.

The man could be sweet when he wanted to be.

She slipped on the panties and bra, which gave her a little thrill because he had picked them out for her to wear. She had never been this intimate with a Dom before, which said a lot about her past relationships. Even with Micah, she had never shared a space like this with him. There were usually one-night stands when she was in town. Now…she liked this. She liked the idea that she could wake up next to Jensen in the morning.

She pushed those feelings away. If she got caught up in daydreaming about what she wanted, she wouldn't be able to enjoy what she had.

After she had the dress on, she looked at herself in the mirror. It was the perfect fit, of course.

"You look beautiful," he said. She hadn't heard him open the door.

She looked at him in the mirror. "You told me the same thing when I was naked."

He smiled as he walked toward her. He stopped when he was standing behind her. "True, but I particularly like seeing you wear something I bought you. Not to mention the lingerie. I know exactly what you are wearing beneath the dress. Gives me a secret little thrill."

She turned. "Same here." She brushed her mouth over his. "Thank you for the dress."

"You are most welcome. Now, time for breakfast."

"Good because I'm starving."

He took her hand and led her out of the room and down the stairs to the lanai. There, beneath the cabana, the table had a place setting for two people. The coffee pot sat in the middle.

"I only get coffee?" she asked chuckling.

"No," he said. "Ah, here is Marta."

"Happy Birthday, Nicola."

"Mahalo, Marta." Then she saw the tray filled with all her favorite tropical fruits, not to mention Marta's macadamia nut pancakes along with coconut syrup. She watched as Marta set the tray on the table. "Oh, that looks delicious. Mahalo."

"You are very welcome. Sit, eat. Enjoy your morning."

She did as Marta ordered. Jensen sat opposite of her, a smug smile curving his lips. He reached for the pancakes and she smacked his hand.

"Who said you get any?"

He looked at her. "I was going to serve you first," he said.

She realized he was serious. "Thank you."

"You're welcome."

"For everything. Not just for this, but the dress, and making sure Marta made this breakfast."

"Well, this is only part of the fun."

"What else do you have planned?"

"How about a drive around the island in a convertible? You always talk about doing that and we never have time."

"That sounds brilliant," she said as she poured coffee into his cup, then hers. "I guess I'll have to put my hair up."

"Yeah, I hate that, because I like to see you wear it down, it cannot be helped, however. Let's eat so we can head out. It's a gorgeous day."

"So, the ride around the island," she said pouring way too much syrup on her pancakes. "What else?"

He smiled. "It's a surprise."

She wanted to push him, but for this one day, she would simply go with the flow and enjoy his plans.

JENSEN WAS SO pleased with how the day was going, but he was a little apprehensive about the next part. He had talked over his plans with Serenity, and she seemed to think they were perfect. In fact, she had seemed positive that Nicola would love them. He took the Salt Lake exit.

"Is the Aloha Stadium Flea Market open today?" she asked looking over in the direction of the stadium.

He shook his head and turned to drive under the overpass. He pulled into a parking lot for a shopping center, his destination right in front of them. He parked in front of the building. She said nothing as she stared at the sign.

"Nicola?"

She looked at him.

"Are you mad?"

She shook her head. "I just don't want to hog the ice."

"I rented out the place for two hours. You get the ice all to yourself."

She blinked. "I don't have my skates or gear."

"In the trunk." When she continued to stare at him, his worry increased. "Say something. We don't have to stay. We can just leave after I tell the owner."

She raised both of her hands to cup his face, then she leaned forward and brushed her mouth over his. When she pulled back, there were tears in her eyes. "Thank you. It's one of the best birthday presents I have ever gotten."

His heart danced. "Yes?"

She nodded. As she wiped at her eyes. "Let's go in so we can hit the ice."

"Oh, no. I'm here to watch you. I've never seen you skate in person."

She frowned. "Really?"

He shook his head.

"Let's go. But once I skate, you are getting your cute ass out there too."

He hoped that wasn't true, because he could not skate to save his life. He slipped out of the car and grabbed the bag from the trunk that he'd packed. It only took ten minutes after they got into the skating rink for her to hit the ice. She was warming up when he gave a song to the manager.

"Nice thing you are doing for her," the manager said.

"It's her birthday and she loves to skate."

"I recognize her." Jensen tore his attention away from Nicola to look at the manager. "Don't worry. I won't tell anyone."

"Thanks."

Then he sat down and watched as she skated around the rink, doing jumps and twirls.

She came over to him. "I wanted to skate to this Sia song."

"I know."

"How do you know?"

"I talked to Serenity. She told me that was your new favorite song to skate to. Just signal the booth when you're ready."

She crooked her finger, urging him closer. She leaned over and kissed him again. "I was serious, you will come skating with me."

"I'm not dressed for it."

"Buy some clothes. I'm sure they have gear."

"That seems frivolous."

She laughed as she skated backward away from him. "You're a billionaire, Jensen. Suck it up."

She went out onto the ice and motioned to the booth. He watched as she moved to Sia's haunting voice as she sang of being unstoppable. He had never been a fan of women's figure skating until he watched video of Nicola. But in person, it was completely different. With each jump, he held his breath until she stuck the landing. And she made every one of them. There was strength in her skating, but he could also see the ballet training. It was why she was so graceful, so amazing even off the ice. The music soared as she sped around the ice, until the perfect spot of the music. She flew through the air, and he found himself holding his breath as she twirled around three times.

She finished the routine off with a fist in the air. For a long moment, there was no sound in the rink, only the echo of the music that had stopped. He didn't know what to say. His mind was still trying to wrap around what he had witnessed. She skated over to him.

"Jensen? Are you okay?"

He nodded. "That was…"

"What?" When he said nothing, she started to babble. "I can't stick those crazy things they are doing today, but I can still do a triple, which is pretty amazing at my age."

He stood. "That was possibly one of the most beautiful things I've watched."

"Really?"

He nodded. She responded with a bright smile. "Thank you. Now, go get some skates buster. We *are* skating."

At that moment, he couldn't deny her anything, so he did her bidding. The Dom in him was pretty damned happy to do as she said, because she had given him a glimpse at perfection.

NICOLA SMILED as Jensen turned onto their street. "This was the most perfect day. Thank you."

He slanted her a look. "I think you were more appreciative of the shrimp truck shrimp than my breakfast."

"You didn't make the breakfast."

He grunted, but she didn't care. The cool, sweet night air danced over her.

"May I ask you a question?"

"You can do anything you like," she said with a laugh.

"You really are in a good mood."

"The two glasses of wine helped."

"Can you tell me why you walked away from it all?" he said as he turned into their drive after the gate opened. "You love to skate."

She sighed as he parked the car.

"Never mind. I don't want you to think about bad things today."

She shook her head. "No. It's okay. Let's just go inside."

He nodded and slipped out of the car. She followed him up the path to the front door and after walking inside, they both slipped off their shoes. She headed to the kitchen and sat on one of the bar stools. He sat beside her.

"I didn't talk about it much at the time or since because… well, I'm not really sure why. At the time it was almost too much. I was so wrecked."

"Did he cheat?"

She shook her head. "Nope. Not really. About a year before the Olympics, Oliver had a bad fall on the ice. He bruised his hip bone and convinced the doctor he needed some strong meds to get him through it. He didn't want me to know. He told me everything was fine."

"But it wasn't?"

She shook her head thinking back to that crazy time in her life. "It didn't happen overnight, but it felt as though it did. We had so much training to do, so many appearances and interviews, I didn't notice that he was popping pills like they were candy."

"He was an addict." Not a question but a statement.

"Yes, and when I found out, I lost it. He promised me it was only for after practice, and I believed him because I was young and stupid."

He brushed the backs of his fingers against her cheek. "And you loved him."

She shrugged. "I thought I did at the time, but again, I was young. He had been my only boyfriend. Our lives were wrapped up in the skating world, and it was all we knew."

She leaned back in the barstool seat.

"Go on," he said.

"That exhibition, our last skate together, he was high. I didn't realize it until we were out on the ice in the middle of our routine. Every toss left me in fear. By the time we got done, I was a mess."

"And you walked away."

"I wanted him to get help. I said we would make a joint statement. He refused and said he didn't have a problem. I gave him an ultimatum, and he told me to go to hell. Those were the last words he said to me."

He took her hand and raised it to his lips. "I'm sorry you had to go through that."

"I am sure you read the rest...or heard it.

"I would rather hear it from you."

"Oliver was convinced I would out him. I was basically going to call his mother and father, and demand that we have an intervention, but I would have never gone to the tabloids." She sighed. "He killed himself that night."

"I'm sorry," he said again.

"It was a long time ago.

"Nevertheless, it had an impact on your life. Is that why you started working as a sober companion?"

She nodded. "In a roundabout way. A year after Oliver's death, my mother made me go to a support group for family and friends of addicts. It was there I realized that much of Oliver's behavior before the drugs had been borderline abusive. It took me awhile to come to terms with that, but once I did, another member approached me and told me I should think about being a sober companion."

"And then a few years later, my mother hired you."

She nodded.

"I truly hate that you went through all of that. It must have been so difficult."

"The aftermath was worse. I was the horrible woman who caused all the problems. His parents attacked me in the press. I went from being America's Sweetheart to the demon woman."

"Come on," he said, as he tugged her off the barstool.

He took her to his room. She expected some extra special play for the night. Instead, he turned her around and pulled the pins out of her hair.

"I obsess about your hair. It's so amazing."

Before she could respond, Jensen turned her around again. Still, no orders. He undressed her slowly, lovingly. With each move, she felt cherished. Her heart seemed lodged in her throat. After pulling off her dress, he undid her bra, bending his head to take first one nipple, then the other into his mouth.

Desire soared as his fingers slipped beneath the waistband of her thong. He bent to help her step out of it, then stayed on his knees. He pressed his mouth against her sex, his tongue slipping inside of her over and over. She settled her hands on his shoulders as he teased her clit with the scrape of his teeth. She leaned her head back, closing her eyes. Arousal twisted with a deeper need, one that she didn't even know she had. To be needed, wanted in this way, to be treated as if she were something precious, all of it entwined with the love she had for him.

He continued to tease her clit as he slid a finger inside of her. He had given her no orders, so as she felt her orgasm approach, she didn't even try to fight it. Electricity sparked as she set her hands against the back of his head to urge him on. She was so close, so damned close. She thought she would never make it to the pinnacle as the heat that had built in her stomach dropped lower. Her legs shook, her body bowed against his mouth, and in the next instant, she screamed his name as she tumbled over the edge into bliss. He kept his mouth against her as she rode out her orgasm. By the time he rose to his feet, she was barely able to stand.

Jensen lifted her into his arms and carried her to the bed. He stripped out of his clothes, then joined her, covering her body with his. The kiss he gave her then was filled with tenderness and need. By the time he pulled back, she had to blink tears away. The man was undoing her with every move he made. She was helpless against the flood of emotion that twisted through her. Love and desire inter-twined and then surrounded her heart.

"What?" he asked.

She shook her head not wanting to burden him. Nicola didn't want to ruin the moment, not now.

Jensen rose to his knees, then lifted her up by her hips. In one fast, hard move, he thrust into her. She was wet enough that it didn't hurt, but she was still sensitive from her release. Even so, she didn't care. This was what she wanted, what she needed right at that particular moment. He started to move inside of her. She had thought she wouldn't be able to come again, but he built up her need once again, pushing her to her limits. His moves were lazy at first, but soon, he was moving faster and harder in and out of her. As he coaxed another orgasm from her, her body bowed up off the bed. She seemed to have no control as he kept moving, teasing her, not allowing her to shy away from what he wanted from her. Again, he built her up, using his cock and his hands. Her release was shimmering just out of her reach when he slipped his hand down to her clit. He pressed hard against it, sending her soaring into another release. He followed her in the next moment as he groaned out her name.

Jensen collapsed on her and she wrapped her arms around him. She loved when he dominated her, but this night would be something she would hold close to her heart forever.

"Oh, bloody hell," he said lifting his head.

"You say the sweetest things to me."

"No, we didn't use a condom."

"Oh. Well, I'm on the pill, so no worries there."

"I've been tested." She knew he meant for AIDS. He had been a heroin addict, so that made sense.

"As I have. I don't think we have anything to worry about."

"Okay." He bent his head and kissed her. It was long, wet, and sweet. "Thank you."

"I should be thanking you," she said, trying her best to keep it light.

"I…I want you to know that you aren't *that* girl."

She blinked. "What?"

"You were never stupid, but you were young and sheltered. He hurt you."

"Jensen—"

"No. I have something to say. I wanted you to know how much I care about you. I wanted you to know just how special you are, that you aren't someone who should have been treated that way. And to know, coming from an addict, that none of it is your fault."

For a long moment, she couldn't say anything. The lump in her throat made it difficult. In the aftermath of Oliver's suicide and the end of her career, no one had said that to her. Not even her parents.

She raised her hand and skimmed her fingers over his cheek. "Thank you."

They stared at each other for a long moment, then he asked, "How about a shower?"

"Sounds divine."

He slipped out of her, then off the mattress. He picked her up again and walked to the bathroom. She had a lot of worries, but right now, none of them seemed to matter.

AFTER THE QUICK SHOWER, Jensen and Nicola had snuggled together. He knew from her even breathing that she was sleeping within five minutes. It had been a long day, and he had made sure he wore her out when they made love.

Jensen didn't know exactly when he decided not to use Domination tonight. It was probably when she had finished her story. He had wanted to do nothing more than to love her. He needed her to know just how special she was.

He was sure he accomplished that, but now he had another problem to solve: How did he convince her that she should take another chance on an addict?

chapter sixteen

The next afternoon, Nicola was sitting on the lanai in the back of Serenity's house. Waves crashed beyond the trees, and she could hear people chattering.

"I hate to leave," she said.

"Then stay."

"I can't. We're supposed to get that new contract, and I need to go over it with Jensen."

Serenity chuckled. "Sure. Pretend like you aren't dumping me for a guy."

"It's daytime."

"Does that mean you have no feelings during daytime?" Nicola said nothing, so Serenity plowed ahead. "Yesterday you spent all day with him, so don't tell me that wasn't during business hours."

"Stop," she said, trying to put enough humor in her voice to deflect Serenity. Her friend was in full-blown ranting mode though, and when Serenity got on a tear, there was no way of stopping her. Nicola didn't have the emotional stability to fight against Serenity's hopeful comments. Nicola knew that if she bought into the possibility of having more than just an affair, she would end up hurt in the end.

"You know, normally I would be okay with your little arrangement if you didn't feel anything for him. But you do. You love him, Nic."

"Serenity—"

"No. Stop it. You act like that's all beneath you."

"It's not that." It wasn't. It was that she thought she wasn't good enough for happily ever after.

"What is it then?"

She sighed. "I don't know if I'm made for long-term relationships. I had one and it was fucked up beyond all recognition by the time it ended."

Nicola expected sympathy, what she got was a verbal kick to the head. "Oh, get over yourself, woman. Good God, most of us have regrettable relationships from our teens. What you have with Jensen is special."

She shook her head. "No, well, maybe for me."

"For Jensen too. Remember, he was here the other day and I talked to him. He planned all of your birthday before he had arrived. He only asked me about the music and arranged when you would arrive here."

"Come on."

"No. He had the whole thing planned. That is not something you do for a friend you've had an arrangement with for only a few weeks. That's a man who is thoroughly smitten."

Serenity took off her sunglasses and looked at Nicola.

"Don't you dare act like it's just another relationship. It isn't. This isn't one of the Dom toys you keep around the world. This is Jensen. This is a man you will have to see every day after you leave this island. You went into this knowing that it would be difficult once it was done. But you did it anyway."

"It is only for our time here. After that, it would be too difficult."

"For you...or him?"

"What do you mean by that?"

"I mean you keep men at arm's length. Seriously, I understand. Oliver was a bastard. But this is a chance for something more, and you are going to toss it away like an idiot. You deserve to be happy, Nic. Take a chance on him."

"And do what? Tell him I want to make this permanent, and I want to have his babies?" she shouted the question, surprising both her and Serenity. "What happens if he says no? How do we go on from there? I will be out of a job because it would be too awkward to continue."

Serenity's eyes softened. "I have a feeling he wouldn't say no."

Nicola shook her head. "I can't take that chance. I might love him, but I also love my job."

"So, you're ready to go back to just being his personal assistant? And before you answer me, think about what that means. You'll make sure he has rides to his favorite BDSM clubs, where he will go play with other women. You can do that now?"

Damn. She hadn't even thought about that.

"I can tell you don't want to do that. Take a chance on him and you. You *are* worth it."

She sighed. "When did you get so smart?"

"I have this friend who told me the same thing not that long ago. It all ended well for me."

Nicola smiled. "Okay. I'll think about it, but right now, I need to get back because I still have a job to do."

She stood, then helped Serenity up out of her lounge

chair. "Pretty soon, getting out of the chair is going to be too hard on me. Oh, hey, what did Jeff want the other day?"

"Oh, God, I forgot to tell you. He and Ben are looking for a surrogate," she said as she followed Serenity into the house. She ran into Serenity's back when she suddenly stopped in her tracks.

"Oof," Nicola said and almost fell backward. Serenity grabbed her, then dropped her hands to settle them on her hips.

"How dare you not tell me about that?"

"Sorry. I've been busy, and Jensen was with me last night. He was not happy when I told him."

"What do you mean?"

"He told me he was worried they were trying to steal me away."

"He *does* know they are just gay, right?"

"Yes. At first, he thought they were trying to hire me to handle the production company business."

"You would be good at it," Serenity said. Nicola shook her head. "You know you would be."

"Yes, but Jeff and I would be at each other's throats. He doesn't take direction well."

Serenity chuckled.

"What?" she asked.

"I just realized you're the Domme during the day and Jensen's the Dom at night."

Nicola rolled her eyes. "Anyway, I'm calling them tomorrow to tell them no."

"Why didn't you tell them that right away?"

"First, because they would not take no for an answer unless I thought it over."

"And second?"

"Okay, I don't want to do it with them, but it wasn't until that moment that I realized how much I wanted a baby."

"That makes sense. Of course, you've always said you might want a child."

"No, not in some abstract way. In a like right now, or in the very near future kind of way. But I didn't want in vitro with a couple of my gay friends. I wanted to have a baby with a man."

"With Jensen," Serenity said quietly. "Talk to him, Nic. You two need to have a long discussion about the future. You know I'm right."

"Fine, you are, but it doesn't mean that I can do it today. I'll get us through the whole stupid contract crap. Then I'll deal with it."

"Just make sure you do, or you might really regret it."

NICOLA WAS STILL THINKING about what Serenity had said as she drove home that afternoon. She knew her friend was right. She needed to have a talk with Jensen, but Nicola knew it would have to wait. This deal was important to the family, especially Lillian. Bringing their personal issues out today would be bad.

Still, she kept remembering the night before, the way he had made love to her had left her feeling out of sorts. She could usually read a Dom, but last night had not been about Domination or even kinky sex. It had been more about showing her he cared about her. The soft touch of his hands and mouth, the way he had sounded when he said her name…

She blinked when she realized she was daydreaming

driving on a twisty road near a cliff. Granted, she was on the inside lane, but there was a lot of traffic. Early afternoon brought out the tourists, who loved to stop at all the scenic viewing spots.

Thankfully, she made it to one of the parts of the drive that didn't have a cliff on her left-hand side for a little while. The traffic light ahead at Kealahou Street turned yellow, and knowing she didn't have time to speed through, she hit her brakes.

Nothing happened. She kept moving forward. Again and again she pressed down on the brake pedal, but still, nothing happened. She was barreling toward the intersection as the light turned red. The other cars started to move through, and she tried her best to swerve to miss them. One hit her back end, sending her spinning. Nicola tried her best to straighten the car out, but in the end, she slammed into the traffic light pole on the opposite side of the street. The barrier didn't hold her, and she rolled down the short incline to the beach.

When the car seemed to settle, she sat there, unsure of what to do. Her head was spinning, and she was shaking. She heard people shouting, then banging on her window. She glanced up and found an older Asian man asking her if she was all right.

She nodded and immediately regretted it. Her brain throbbed.

"Let me help you out of there," he said. He opened her door and held out his hand. "I'm sorry I hit you."

She blinked as she grabbed her purse, then took his hand. "It wasn't your fault. My brakes went out. I kept hitting them and nothing happened. The fault was mine."

"We called 911," he said as he helped her around to the back end of her car. "Are you sure you're okay?"

"My head is a little rattled, but other than that, I'm fine. You said you called 911?"

He nodded.

"I need to call my boss to let him know. Did you see my purse?"

"You're holding it," he said, frowning at her.

She shook her head. "No worries. I'm just a little shaken up."

It was then she saw his car sitting on the side of the road.

"I am so sorry about this," she said. "I will make sure everything is taken care of. You won't have to pay a dime."

He nodded. "I'm going to go keep a look out for the cops. Are you sure you're okay?"

"I'm fine, thank you."

As he walked up the sandy hill, she hit Jensen's number and hoped he didn't freak out too much.

JENSEN'S HEART was still in his throat as he arrived at the accident site. The cops had arrived and were directing traffic, but the moment he saw the ambulance, he almost lost all calm. He drove past the accident, then parked off the side of the road. He waited to let a couple of cars drive past him, then he got out of the car and walked to the scene. He saw her then, sitting in the back of the ambulance. She had an EMT jacket on for some reason, as one of them was patching her up.

"Sir, only cops are allowed past here," a young uniformed cop said.

"That's my girlfriend," he said pointing toward the ambulance. "I want to see her."

The younger man nodded and let him past. As he walked toward her, he realized what he had just said. His girlfriend. She wasn't that. She worked for him. He didn't want a girlfriend, especially not her. If he was going to keep her beyond her job, he would definitely marry her.

He stopped walking and tried to gather his thoughts. He wanted to marry her, and he wanted her in his life. Forever. And not just for work or for sex. He didn't want something temporary.

He'd had those thoughts before, but not until he thought he might have lost her did Jensen realize that it wasn't a fantasy. Now, he wanted it to be his reality. Just like last night, he knew it would take a lot of convincing.

The sound of the tow truck brought him out of his thoughts. He started back on the path to her.

"Jensen," she said, her voice wavering a bit. He could tell she was trying to hold it together, but she was seriously close to losing it.

"I think you could have come up with a better way to avoid a video conference than plowing into another car."

She gave him a sad smile.

"Is there anything wrong with her? Can she go home?" he asked the EMT.

He shook his head. "She's fine. No signs of concussion, but she should rest tonight."

"I'll make sure of it. Come on, love. I'll take you home."

"I need to talk to Ms. McCann first," someone said from behind him. A uniformed cop had a pen and pad out.

"She needs rest," Jensen insisted.

"I need to tell him what happened, Jensen. It's better if I do it now while it's fresh in my memory, right?" she asked the cop.

He nodded and handed her his card. "My name is Officer Tanaka. Can you tell me what happened?"

She nodded. "I came up to the intersection and the light turned yellow. When I hit my brakes, nothing happened."

"What do you mean?" Tanaka asked.

"The brakes. They didn't work. My car just kept moving ahead."

"When was the last time you had the brakes checked?"

"I don't know. It's a rental."

"What company?" he asked. Jensen rattled off the company's name.

"I need your contact info because we will probably need to talk again," he said.

"Where's my purse. I have cards in there."

Jensen spotted it behind her in the ambulance. He grabbed it.

"Where?"

"I have a card holder in there. I can get it."

"You will sit there and let me find it."

She didn't look happy about it, but she did as he ordered. He found them easily and handed them to Tanaka. "We are going to be here for another week, but she can be reached at that number. If we need to stay longer, just let us know."

"Of course, sir. I hope you're feeling better, Ms. McCann."

"Mahalo," she said. He smiled and made his way back to the other officers.

"You said the brakes went out?"

She nodded, then winced.

"What?"

"My head and neck hurt. I didn't hit anything, but I am still a little out of it."

"Let's go home."

"Yes. I could do with a long soak in the tub."

She slipped off the jacket and handed it to the EMT. "Mahalo."

He led her up the sandy hill, trying his best not give into the urge to lift her into his arms and carry her. Nicola would not appreciate that. He helped her into the car.

"Give me a second. I want to give them my card too," he said. She really was out of it because she only nodded, then closed her eyes and leaned back against the seat. He was just glad that he had kept the convertible from the rental company for another day, so he hadn't had to show up in the limo.

"Tanaka," he said. The officer turned.

"Did you need something?"

"Yes. Here is my card. I'm going to make sure she rests and that means stealing her phone and hiding it. If you need anything, call me. Tomorrow she will be back in fighting form, but today she needs to rest."

"Of course," he said taking the card.

"Does it mean something that the brakes went out?"

Tanaka shrugged. "Could just be that the rental company didn't keep up the maintenance, but that seems odd for them, especially for the luxury cars like that one. We'll investigate, which will mean sending the car to have it inspected, especially the brakes. We will figure out what went wrong."

"Thanks." He made his way back to the car and it struck him. She had driven along that road in the morning, the twists where cars were dangerously close to the edge. If the brakes had gone out that morning, she might have gone over the edge. He could have lost her.

He stopped at the back of his car, waiting again for other vehicles to drive by. Once he got in, he looked over at Nicola.

She was sleeping. At least that was something. He started up the engine and pulled out when the road was clear.

One thing was certain, he would find out what happened and whoever was at fault would pay.

THE NEXT MORNING, Nicola was sitting at the bar in the kitchen when the doorbell rang. She frowned.

"Are we expecting anyone?" she asked loud enough for Jensen to hear in his office.

He stepped out and headed in the direction of the front door. "Not that I know of."

She heard the murmur of male voices, then Jensen reappeared with a man walking behind him.

"Nicola, this is Detective Rome Carino."

She studied the man. He was as tall as Jensen, but where Jensen was lean like a swimmer, Carino was built like a linebacker.

"Good morning. Would you like some coffee?"

"No, thanks. I wanted to talk to you about your accident yesterday."

"Why don't we go into the living room?" Jensen suggested.

"That sounds good," Carino said.

Jensen took her hand and led her into the living area, like she was an invalid. He had been treating her that way since she came home the day before, and it was starting to piss her off. Still, she said nothing because she couldn't forget the look on his face when she first saw him at the accident scene the day before. His haunted expression had told her he was more shaken up about her accident than she was.

After they settled on one couch, Carino sat on the opposite one.

"Before we begin, I thought you might explain why a homicide detective is here to talk to us," Jensen said.

"What?" she asked, and Jensen showed her Carino's business card.

"It's what we found and because I got a call from Conner Dillon."

"The man who handled our security at the house?" she asked.

"Yeah, we have a history and similar interests. Anyway, when the word came down about the car, we thought we should handle this one differently."

"What the bloody hell are you talking about?"

"The brake lines had been cut."

It took her a second to absorb that information.

"The brake lines?" Jensen asked. "You're saying someone did it on purpose."

"Yes, and whoever it was did it well. Are you the main driver of the car, Ms. McCann?"

She nodded. "Since we rented it when we arrived."

"So, tell me," Carino said. "Who wants you dead?"

chapter seventeen

For a long moment, neither he nor Nicola responded to the absurd question.

"Kill me?" Nicola asked, her voice sounded so small. Jensen slipped his arm around her and pulled her closer.

"Yes. We found a tiny hole in the brake line. It tells us that either the person didn't know what they were doing, or they were very crafty."

"Why would that make them crafty?" Jensen asked.

"It means they knew it would be a slow leak, so they would be safely out of the area. Seeing where you had your accident tells me you were very lucky."

She nodded. "I drove to my friend Serenity's house that morning in the opposite direction."

Her voice shook, and he pulled her closer. Jensen hated this. He hated the entire situation.

"I hear that you're here for some business."

He nodded. "We're negotiating a deal with the Johnson family on Maui."

"You're buying them out?"

"No, they are making us minority partners, which allows us to invest some money and then have the possibility to make money later."

"Was anyone protesting? The Hawaiians take their land very seriously, especially these last few years."

"No."

"Oh, but what about Michael?" Nicola asked.

"Who?"

"Michael Johnson. He is Robert's son. He was definitely opposed to the deal."

Before they could continue, the doorbell rang.

"Bloody Grand Central in here today," he said as he went to the front door. He didn't know exactly what was going on, but he refused to believe anyone would want to hurt Nicola.

When he looked through the peephole, he saw Alfie. He opened the door.

"What the bloody hell are you doing here?"

"Sorry, I stopped by because I heard what happened with Nicola. Is she okay?"

"Yes, although I'm not sure for how long. How did you get in?"

"The gate was open. I made sure it closed when I came through."

Dillon had given Carino the code, so Jensen assumed he left the gate open. "Come on in. How did you find out?"

"I came over this morning from Maui, but I checked in with the Johnsons. They told me."

He led Alfie back to the living room, but there was a part of him who didn't want Alfie there. He felt guilty for it. Not because of their friendship, but because he knew Alfie was harmless. He'd lost most of his friends when his father had lost their money, so Jensen had gone out of his way to stay on friendly terms with him.

"Nicola, I just found out and came over," he said, taking Jensen's seat next to Nicola. Jensen did everything he could to control the growl vibrating in his throat. Nicola had made it clear in the past that Alfie was not to her taste, but Jensen still didn't like him sitting next to Nicola.

He got a look from Carino that told Jensen he knew of his interest in Nicola. He made a motion with his head.

When he stood, Nicola said, "Wait, do you need to talk about this more?"

"I'm going to give him the contact details for Michael. We'll be right back."

The glare she sent his way meant he was going to pay for this.

"Are you talking about Michael Johnson?" Alfie asked.

"Yes," Jensen said. "It's a long shot since he lives on Maui."

"But I saw him here. He was down hanging out at the Wailana Coffee House this morning. He said he was staying at the Hilton."

"You talked to him?" Nicola asked.

"Yes. You think he had something to do with this?"

She opened her mouth, but Carino stopped her. "We're going to talk to him, that's for sure, but I don't want to jump to any conclusions."

"Of course."

"You said he's at the Hilton?"

Alfie nodded.

"I'll have some officers go down there and make sure he stays put so I can question him."

"I want to go too," Jensen said.

Carino shook his head. "I really don't think that is a good idea."

"Either I go with you or I follow you."

He wasn't happy with the situation, but Carino was smart enough to know that Jensen meant what he said.

"Alfie, do you mind staying here with Nicola?"

"Sure," he replied.

"I can take care of myself."

He sighed. The woman was a pain in the arse a lot of the time. It was probably one of the reasons he loved her.

"May I have a word with you?"

She frowned, and if they had been alone, she probably would have told him to bugger off. But, with the audience, she behaved. She rose and followed him into the foyer where they had a little privacy.

"I don't need to worry about you."

"I can take care of myself. My father taught me how to defend myself."

"Did he now?"

She nodded. "He didn't like that *Ma*ma and I were out on our own. He wanted to make sure I could defend myself no matter what the situation."

"Even so, I would feel better if he were here."

"I wouldn't," she said.

"Why not?"

"I know he's your friend, but he gives me the creeps. It makes me feel bad to admit."

"We'll only be an hour or so, then I can come back and kick him out." He took her hand and pulled her into his arms.

She smiled at him. "Okay."

He knew it probably wasn't a good idea, but he bent his head and kissed her. He meant for it to only be a simple kiss, but he felt himself falling fast. It didn't matter where they were when he kissed her, he didn't seem to be able to keep it sweet. Instead, he wanted to devour her. For once, he listened to his better instincts and ended the kiss.

He heard a sound and glanced over to see Carino waiting on them. "We'll be back before you know it."

She nodded, and he kissed her forehead. She walked with them to the door and waited until they both got into Carino's car before closing it.

"So, along with the call I got from Dillon, I got one from Ross," Carino said as he started the car.

"That's where I have seen you before. I take it you're a member?"

He nodded. "My wife and I both are."

"Ah." Jensen glanced at the detective. "I would appreciate it if you keep things about my relationship with Nicola quiet."

"Trying to keep it secret?"

"For now. I just don't need the irritation my family would cause if it leaked out to the press."

"They don't approve of her?"

"Good God no. My mother would be thrilled and would start pressuring both of us. Plus, we have other issues."

"Unless there is a reason for it to come out in the investigation, I see no reason why it should be an issue."

"Good. Now," he said, as Carino headed toward the heart of Waikiki, "let's go find this bastard."

BY THE TIME they arrived at the hotel, Michael was already detained in his room by a couple of HPD officers. When they walked into the room, Michael's face was white as the sheets on his bed. He looked like he had sweat out enough moisture to fill the Super Pool at the Hilton.

Anger shifted through Jensen. He curled his fingers into the palms of his hands as he tried to ignore the need to beat the man to a bloody pulp. He lunged forward, unable to really control his rage, but Carino stopped him and pushed him away.

"I don't want to have to arrest you for assault."

"I should have known you were behind this," Michael spat out.

"Why would you say that?" Carino asked.

"He's trying his best to get control of my family's resort."

"You're an idiot," Jensen said. "We already have a verbal agreement, and I would have signed the papers if you hadn't tried to kill Nicola."

"Nicola? You mean Ms. McCann? Why would I want to hurt her?"

"You thought it might help your cause."

Carino shook his head and motioned for Jensen to step back. He did, but he started to pace in the small space. It was the best he could do now.

"What are you doing on Oahu?"

He glanced at Jensen. "I came here to meet the VP."

Jensen stopped pacing. "Alfie? Why would you meet with him here?"

"He's been here for days. I came over because he said he had a way to save my resort, plus stick it to you. That man doesn't like you, bruddah."

"What the hell are you talking about?" Jensen said approaching him. Carino stepped neatly in his way.

"He doesn't like Wulf?"

"No, hates him more than I do." He leaned over so he

could make eye contact with Jensen. "He wants to see you ruined."

Carino looked at him. "Could this be true?"

"I don't see how." He looked at Michael. "Are you sure?"

He nodded. "Truth is, I thought he wanted to ruin you financially, not hurt Ms. McCann. I wouldn't be okay with that."

Carino's phone buzzed. He looked at the number. "I have to take this."

He stepped away and Jensen moved closer to Michael. Calmer now, he tried to think through the last few years with Alfie. Was what Michael saying right? Did Alfie hate him? He had never done anything wrong, other than the usual boyhood pranks. Hell, he gave Alfie a job when he needed it.

"Are you sure he said these things to you?"

Michael nodded. "That's why Dad didn't want to work with him. He said he couldn't be trusted."

"Wulf, we have a problem. Michael, these officers are staying here until we get this all cleared up."

"Am I under arrest?"

"If that's what keeps you here, then yes, you are."

Carino walked out the door leaving Jensen to jog to keep up with him.

"What's going on?"

The detective pushed the button for the lift. He held up his phone. It was the parking lot at the Aloha Tower Marketplace. He watched it for only a second when he saw Alfie approach the rental car, then slip beneath it.

"The bastard."

"Yeah. They sent it over to see if it was Michael. Call her. Now."

He started calling her, but her phone kept going to voicemail. If he had been worried yesterday, it didn't compare to the terror he felt chilling his blood now.

"Fuck me," he said as they stepped onto the lift. "Nicola, it was Alfie who screwed with your brakes. Carino and I are on the way."

He heard Carino order more cops and an ambulance.

"Dammit. She didn't want him there. Told me he bothered her."

"We'll get there in time," Carino assured him.

"Is that why you ordered the ambulance?"

"I never leave anything to chance. Just pray that he hasn't realized that we know about him."

And for the first time in a long time, Jensen did just that.

NICOLA COULDN'T SEEM to calm her nerves. She'd felt jumpy and irritated since Jensen had left with the detective. She would like to blame it on the situation and not her companion. They were still sitting in the living room watching TV, but she had sat on the couch opposite of his. There was always something off about Alfie. Since first meeting him, she didn't trust him. She knew that he wasn't that happy when Jensen got clean. He would pretend, but every now and then, he would make an offhand remark that told her he was a user. Part of it was his behavior toward Julienne. She had told Nicola that he had tried to hit on her when she was barely seventeen years old. Jules tried to steer clear of him ever since. That should have told her something.

Nicola looked at the clock and realized she didn't know where her phone was. Jensen had taken it away the day before, so she would sleep, but she wanted it now. Rising, she started toward his office That would be the one place she thought Jensen would keep her phone. She found it on his desk, but it was turned off, so she booted it on.

"What are you doing?" Alfie said from the doorway.

She jumped and turned around. "Oh, Alfie. Wow, you scared me a little. I guess it's because I am so jumpy since the accident yesterday."

She saw a voicemail from Jensen from about fifteen minutes earlier. Clicking it on, she listened. *Nicola, it was Alfie who screwed with your brakes. Carino and I are on the way.*

She looked at Alfie and knew in that moment, he understood what had just happened. He pulled a small revolver out of his jacket pocket.

"I really hate that it has come to this."

"Why?"

"Why do I hate that it came to this, or why am I going to shoot you?"

"Why are you going to shoot me?"

"Simple. It will hurt Jensen."

"They know it's you."

"I gathered that from your expression. But, at this point, I don't really care. Right now, I just want to make him suffer."

"Why? What did he ever do to you?"

"He treated me like an outsider," he said, his voice rising just a little. She knew if she could get him distracted by talking about himself, she might be able to get away or at least charge him.

"An outsider? How, by giving you a job?"

"No. At Wulf, only family members get the higher positions."

"You are VP of Acquisitions. Did you really think you would get CEO?" she asked, inching closer.

"He was always talking down to me," he continued

ignoring her question. "The man treated me like a subordinate."

"You *are* a subordinate. You work for him."

"I'm better than him. My father made his millions on his own."

"And from what I understand, he lost it all on his own too."

"You bitch," he screamed.

"And why all this hatred toward me? What did I do?"

"You helped him stay clean. Even when I came to New York while you were gone, and we went out, you took care of him. You are the one he needs, always. You don't think I know you've started an affair." He snorted. "Jensen was never that good at hiding his feelings. He's been half in love with you for years, but the way he acted today told me all I needed to know."

"So, you're going to kill me and then what? Kind of hard to get away on an island." She inched even closer, and he still didn't notice. He was so insistent on explaining himself to her that he paid no attention to what she was really doing.

"I don't give a flying fuck what happens. I just know he will suffer. Hell, he would probably start using again, and that would be a just reward, especially since I took him on his first trip."

She blinked. "What?"

"I helped him score his first hit of heroin. Did Jensen not tell you? It was so easy really. He was drowning in all the responsibility of running the company when dear old dad died, so I took him out. Easy enough to get him hooked."

Rage filled her as Alfie's confession sunk in. They hadn't been out partying together, that she could forgive. Alfie had known that Jensen already had a problem with drinking and hooking him on heroin would be easy.

"You bastard," she screamed and rushed him. Alfie was ready for her though. The gun went off and she felt the searing heat of the bullet as it passed through her right shoulder. She ignored it and kept on until she could grab him. He smacked her across the face, and she temporarily lost hold of him. She tasted blood, but again, she paid no attention to the pain. She grabbed him once more and kneed him in the groin, then took him down on the floor. Nicola got hold of his wrist and slammed it until he released the gun. It slid across the floor out of his reach. She punched him, ignoring the searing pain in her shoulder. The crack of his nose bone under her fist had him howling.

Blood spurted, and he screamed. "You broke my nose, you bitch."

Sirens sounded in the distance, and all of a sudden there were hands on her pulling her off of him. With what strength she had left, she tried to fight off whoever it was, but then she heard Jensen's voice and realized it was him.

"Hey, love, come on. Carino will take care of him."

She let him pull her into his arms. "He's a bastard."

"He is." Then hugged her close, causing a shaft of pain to radiate from where she had been shot. She whimpered and he pulled away. "What's wrong?"

The room was starting to spin. "My shoulder."

Jensen apparently hadn't noticed her wound. "What happened? You were shot?"

"Jensen, I'm really dizzy." The room sped up around her as she felt herself falling into a dark abyss. Then she remembered nothing at all.

chapter eighteen

Nicola woke to the sound of Jensen's voice and a beeping. She breathed in the scent of antiseptic and frowned. What happened?

"It doesn't matter why I need it, Mother. Do you have it with you?"

She forced her eyes open and for a second, she didn't know where she was. Jensen was on his cell, but there was little light in the room. As her eyes adjusted, she recognized the room. She had been brought there after recovery the night before. She noticed the sun was trying to peek out from behind the curtains. Yes, it had to be the next day.

She settled her gaze on Jensen again. He had turned away from her and was muttering into the phone, then he hung up. He lowered his head and sighed. He looked worn out, as if he had been through the worst experience of his life. She wanted to give him comfort, cross the room and slip her arms around his waist, but she knew she couldn't. Standing was out of the question.

"Jensen," she said, her voice coming out rough. Damn, her throat was dry.

He turned around and rushed to the bed. Relief softened his features, but it did not hide the fact that he was tired. Dark circles marred the skin beneath his eyes, and he looked as if he had been through hell.

"Are you okay?" she asked.

He gave her a smile as he took her hand, then sat on her bed. "I should be the one asking that. I'm fine, although I'm not made for sleeping in chairs." He brought her hand to his mouth and brushed it over her knuckles.

"What happened? It's all very blurry."

"You were shot."

"By Alfie?"

He nodded. It was then that the flood of memories came rushing back. The fight, the gun going off, her punching him...

"Is Alfie here?"

He shook his head. "They brought him here, patched him up, then Detective Carino booked him. He's going to be in jail a long time."

"Oh."

"Do you remember anything about yesterday?"

"Yes, bits and pieces. He's so jealous of you. He kept ranting about how you stole stuff from him." She closed her eyes as the memories left her a little dizzy. Opening her eyes, she found Jensen staring. "What?"

"You lost a lot of blood. They were very worried about it."

"Everything turned out fine. I'm made of good stock," she said trying to smile. Her cheek hurt from the effort.

"How bad does my face look?" she asked.

Jensen smiled. "Not bad at all now that you're awake. It's been a long eighteen hours."

"Eighteen hours? God, did you talk to the press? Did you—"

"Stop. Things are being taken care of for right now. Mother is in charge of all media issues, so you know it will be handled. She and my brother are on their way here."

"Your mother? God. To Hawaii?"

He shook his head. "To the hospital. I told them to go to the house, but you know Mother."

Oh, crap. His mother, here. She probably looked like hell, and she would more than likely want a rundown of everything. Nicola had no idea what had happened since she'd been asleep.

Then it hit her. "My parents. I've got to get hold of them—"

"Woman, I took care of everything. That was the first call I made. You were shot and have been out for hours. Do you think I can't make a few calls? Serenity and her men will be here later." His frown darkened. "Don't you think I can handle it?"

Her mouth opened, then she snapped it shut. She heard the frustration in his voice, but there was a thread of fear that slinked its way through the words.

"I'm sorry," she said, as she tried to blink back tears.

"Oh, Nic, don't cry. It might just break me," he said in a voice that told her he didn't really want to admit it. "I'm sorry I yelled."

She shook her head as her vision wavered. "No, you're right. You can handle it.

He leaned down and rested his forehead against hers. "I thought I'd lost you. I saw all the blood and…" he stopped talking, apparently unable to continue.

"You should know better than that, Jensen. Nicola is no shrinking flower," Micah said.

She had been so caught up in her conversation with Jensen, she hadn't noticed that the door had opened.

"Can I have some water, Jensen?" she asked. He nodded and filled a cup that had a straw in it. He held it out to her to drink. The cool liquid eased the rawness in her throat.

"Thank you."

"You kind of look banged up," Micah said.

"Screw you, Micah," she said.

He smiled and glanced at Jensen. "You don't look much better."

"Try sleeping in one of those chairs."

"Yeah, not very comfortable, although the maternity ward has recliners so it's a little better."

"What are you doing here, Ross?" Jensen asked, irritation and defensiveness filling his tone.

She glanced at him as he took hold of her hand. Then it hit her. This was the first time they had come face-to-face since Jensen had learned Micah was her first Dom. Was he jealous? No, he couldn't be. Jensen didn't get jealous over his subs. Besides, Micah was crazy in love with his wife.

"I'm friends with Rome Carino. He's a member of Rough 'n Ready, and he knew that we're friends. He let me know what happened and got me in here." He looked at Nicola. "You're going to have to give him a statement, but he said it could wait. That idiot Thompson is still bitching about the right hook you landed on him."

"I kicked him in the nuts too. Did he talk about that?" she asked.

Jensen turned to her, his eyebrows rising. "You did?"

She nodded and instantly regretted it. Pain radiated from her forehead, then spread through her entire skull. Damn.

"Yes. It's one of the many things my father taught me."

He smiled and kissed her knuckles again. "Good."

The door opened and almost hit Micah. From the outfit the woman wore, she assumed it was a nurse. Right behind her was another woman. "Hello, I'm Doctor Jacobs. How are you feeling?"

"Like I've been shot."

The doctor smiled, then looked first at Micah, then Jensen. "You both need to leave. I need to examine the patient. Come back in about twenty minutes."

The sour expression on Jensen's face told her that he wasn't happy about it, but he didn't argue. He let go of her hand and leaned down to brush his mouth over hers.

"I'll be back in a bit."

"Good," she said pulling a smile from him.

"Come on, Wulf, let's go have some coffee. I have a feeling you need it," Micah said, as he followed him out of the room. He gave Nicola a wink, telling her he would look out for Jensen.

"Wulf? As in the Royal Bad Boy? Also known as Bad Boy Billionaire?" the doctor asked.

"He was never a royal," she said. "But yes, that one."

"I thought he looked familiar. Quite the catch," she remarked.

"He's not mine."

"Oh, really? The way he raged last night at me and the rest of the staff, I thought he was your husband."

"No, just a friend. And I work for him. He was just worried about me."

The doctor shook her head. "The man who threatened me last night was not doing that for an employee."

"I apologize. He can be a bit autocratic if I'm not around to control him."

The doctor shook her head. "I think you two have a lot to

talk about, and I'm glad to say you'll be able to accomplish that, thanks to me."

JENSEN AND MICAH barely talked as they ordered their coffees and sat in the cafeteria. Once they were seated, Micah kept staring at him.

"What?" Jensen asked, still irritated with his presence.

"I'm here because my wife told me it was a good idea, and I can see that she was right."

"What the bloody hell do you mean?"

"Don't push yourself too hard. You have friends on the island who can help until your mother gets here."

"And Nicola's mother and father. They will be here later tomorrow, hopefully. The weather is causing a bit of a problem."

"You're flying them here?"

He nodded and took a sip of coffee.

"So, how much do you want to hit me?" Micah asked.

"Because you didn't tell me you were her first Dom?"

Micah nodded.

"Right now, I don't have the energy, but I would like to kick your arse."

He smiled. "You can try, son, but I don't think you would get close. And, I couldn't tell you. It was her right to tell you, not mine."

"Rubbish."

"No. Not really. You didn't know her back then. That relationship…the fucker she skated with was a real bastard. He had her doubting everything. Her ability to skate, her attractiveness, her ability to be a productive human in society. You've talked about it with her? You know what happened?"

He nodded. "I watched the video again and now I see the signs. At first, I didn't see it because when I watched them skate, I always watched Nicola. But after she told me, I re-watched the video. During that last skate, it was easy to see he was high. She could have easily died then."

"Yeah, but she didn't."

"She could have died last night, and it would have been my fault."

"Stop that crap, Wulf. The whole world doesn't revolve around you. And we all thought it was one of those John-sons. Thompson made sure of it."

"I brought him into her world."

"Good God, get over yourself. You Brits are always so damned proper. Alfie Thompson is an asshole, who is going to spend a long time in jail."

Jensen nodded but he wasn't convinced.

"If you are so sure that you're a danger to her, maybe you need to let her go."

Anger swept through him. "Over my dead body."

Micah smiled. "Good. She's good for you, but you're also good for her. I'm glad you found each other." When Jensen didn't say anything, Micah asked, "You *are* planning on a permanent D/s relationship, right?"

"Kind of."

"What the hell does that mean?" he demanded, and it made Jensen smile. He sounded like an outraged father.

"I have even more permanent plans, as long as she doesn't screw them up," Jensen said. "Do you know she wanted to call the press when she woke up? She was worried how it would all play out."

"I know you probably already know this, but that's why

she is the perfect sub. She's a control freak, but the type that needs to give it up with someone she trusts."

"Are you giving me a backhanded compliment?"

"Look how smart you are. Yes. I am. She trusts you. More than she ever trusted me. I talked to her in those early days she worked with you. She never used your name, but she always had complete belief in your ability to overcome the addiction. Even after the one setback. Her faith in you always worried me until I met you. I knew then what you both just figured out. You need each other."

"Is this where you say we complete each other?"

He smiled. "No. You already know that. Seeing you together, just those few minutes in the room upstairs showed me."

He sighed. "I still can't believe I almost lost her."

"Need a hit?"

"What?"

"Hey, we all know how you met Nicola, and the entire world has access to your drug days via the internet. I would think that you would be jonesing for a hit right about now."

He did also, but it never came. The need to escape, to control his world, it wasn't there.

"No."

Micah cocked his head to the side and studied him. "Really?"

"Surprised the hell out of me too."

"That's good." He studied Jensen another moment. "I know exactly how you're feeling."

"I highly doubt that."

He snorted. "When I met Dee, she was on the run from her father, who had put a hit out on her. I almost lost her too. Hell, when her brother kidnapped her, I worried I *had* lost her."

"Her brother?"

"Devon Stryker, also in hiding because of the hit his father had out on him." Jensen's expression must have shown his thoughts. The club owner smiled. "Yeah. Who would have thought that the bastard son of a whore would be a better catch? Either way, I lived through hell. Each second that ticked by, I felt as if I would lose my shit. Until I finally found her, then almost lost her again. Damned family." He shook his head. "But I ended up with Dee, so I'd do it all over again. Just as I am sure you would."

He sighed and nodded.

"Have you told her?"

"Told her what?" Jensen asked, pretending not to understand the question.

"That you're in love with her."

"Not yet. I had planned on it, but some asshole tried to kill her."

"Get it done soon, son. That woman is in love with you, but she's going to believe your stupid end date to the relationship."

"How the hell do you know about that?"

"She told me. Get irritated and jealous and get over it. Right now, you have to convince the woman that you're in love with her, and that you want forever."

"I have a plan."

Micah rolled his eyes. "Just don't wait too long."

"Why?"

"Women get stupid ideas in their heads. Nicola doesn't usually do that, but she's a woman who has to be busy, and she's going to spend a lot of time recovering. Lots of thinking time."

"Bloody hell."

"Exactly. And don't ever tell my wife I said women get stupid ideas."

"Well, as soon as I talk to her father, I'll propose. Mother's bringing my grandmother's engagement ring that she left to me."

"Good lord, sometimes I forget you're from money."

"That's probably the nicest thing anyone has ever said to me. Well, the second nicest."

"What was the first?"

"When I woke up after the bender that broke my year of sobriety, Nicola was sitting beside my bed in the hospital."

"They let sober companions hang out in rehab?"

"No. I almost overdosed. She made sure that didn't make the papers," he said. "Nicola had been visiting her parents, and…no reason to go into all of that. Anyway, I woke up, and she said, 'Do you want to die? If you do, tell me now and I will find a way to kill you.'"

"That was nicer than what I said?" Micah asked. "You two are weird."

Jensen shook his head. "I, of course, told her I wanted to live. Then, she said, 'Good, because I think you have a lot to offer the world, and I aim to make sure you're sober enough to accomplish that.'" He took a swallow of coffee. "I thought she would walk out, but there she was by my side, ready to fight for me if I told her. I don't know if anyone had ever done that for me before."

"The woman is one of a kind." He chuckled again, then let out a booming laugh. "Still, it is just like her to tell you she'd help kill you if you wanted to die."

Jensen smiled. "I didn't realize it at the time, but I think that's when I started falling for her."

Micah shook his head. "God, you *are* made for each other."

HE AND MICAH made it off the elevator when he heard his mother's voice.

"I don't care. I want to know where my future daughter-in-law is."

"Maybe we should go back down to the cafeteria," he said.

"Why?" Micah asked.

"You're about to meet the reason why." They turned the corner. There stood his mother, dressed as if she had just attended Queen Elizabeth's tea party. Not one blonde hair was out of place. Her blue suit didn't have a single wrinkle. And she was wearing hose and heels. So odd to see that in Hawaii.

Beside her stood his brother, who wore a wrinkled suite and looked ready to fall down. None of them—including their father—had ever been able to keep up with Lillian Wulf.

"Mother," he said. His mother turned to him. That's when he saw her worried expression and the dark circles beneath her eyes.

She rushed forward, his brother trailing behind her. "Jensen."

She threw her arms around him, and he smelled it then. The familiar scent of Chanel No. 5. It was a scent he would always associate with his mother, and it always brought him comfort.

"I am so glad you are safe."

She pulled back and then looked over at Micah.

"Mother, this is Micah Ross. He's a friend."

Micah held out his hand to her. When she put her hand in his, he brought it to his mouth and kissed it. "It is very nice to meet you, Mrs. Wulf."

That slow, southern accent rolled over the words, and his mother actually blushed. His almost sixty-year-old mother.

"Stop that," Jensen said.

"Who are you talking to?" Micah asked.

"Both of you. Go away, Ross."

"Jensen," his mother said, irritation and embarrassment filling her tone. "I will not have you behave so badly. Really."

"No worries, Mrs. Wulf. I hope to see you before you leave our island."

Once he stepped back on the elevator and the door closed, Jensen turned to his brother and mother. "What were you doing at the desk?"

"I couldn't remember the hospital room number."

He frowned and looked at Jakob. His eyes were barely opened.

"I sent you the room number via text."

She was a woman who lived for details, who needed to be in control. For a long moment, he realized that was a quality that both she and Nicola shared. Still, it wasn't forgetful. It wasn't a big issue, but from the mortified look on her face, it was to her.

"I apologize."

"No need."

The only time she had gotten forgetful and scatterbrained was when their father had been sick.

He held out his arm. "What are you wearing?" she asked, taking it.

"These are scrubs. I didn't have a choice because...my other clothes were ruined. Before we go in the room—"

"Why were you out here and not in there with her?"

"The doctor wanted to examine her, and they chased me out. Now, I want your promise you won't make a comment about the ring, and no more of this future daughter-in-law."

"Why not?"

"We aren't engaged. I haven't had time to ask her. So, mum's the word. She knows you are on the island and will be thrilled to see you."

His brother snorted. Jensen shot him a nasty look over his shoulder.

When he knocked on the door, then opened it, his heart almost tumbled out of his chest. She was still in the same position, but it was obvious they'd had her up out of the bed. Her hair had been combed and she had changed gowns.

"Look who I found in the hallway," he said, smiling.

"Mrs. Wulf. Jakob," Nicola said, trying to smile back, then wincing. Her bruised cheek and split lip didn't make it easy for her. "I'm so glad to see you."

"Oh, Nicola," his mother said, releasing his arm and running to her side. His mother leaned down for a hug. She straightened and tsked. "I never liked that Alfie."

"This is the first I'm hearing that," he said.

"Jakob, bring me that chair," his mother ordered.

"Of course," his brother said as he picked up a chair from the other side of the room and brought it over to Nicola's bedside.

His mother sat down in the chair as though she were sitting in attendance with the queen, which she had a few times. Still, after the long trip over, any other person would slouch, like his brother was doing in the chair he had settled in. But Lillian Wulf did not slouch.

"When Jensen called us, I can't tell you how terrified we all were. Julienne wanted to come, but she had a meeting in

France. I told her she could come if Jensen lied about how bad your injuries were."

"Oh, no worries there," Nicola said. "I really didn't expect you to fly all the way over here."

"Of course we came. You are part of our family," his mother said, her voice wavering a little. She reached out and patted Nicola's hand. "I will take care of you until your mother can get here. I owe her that much."

Nicola looked at him, confusion filled her gaze. Then she turned back to his mother. "Thank you. I know she would appreciate it."

His mother gave her one last pat, then she sat back and looked over at him. "You need a shower and a change of clothes. Do that, and we will stay here with Nicola until you return."

He frowned. "I can stay."

"I didn't say you couldn't, but you smell, and well, you look horrible. Go get freshened up."

And that was that. When Lillian Wulf threw out an order, as one of her children, he was helpless but to do as she wished.

"Of course."

He wanted to kiss Nicola goodbye, and he didn't give a damn who saw them, but he knew Nicola wouldn't be happy.

"I'll be back as soon as I can. Rome Carino might come by to talk to you."

She nodded. "I think I'm going to nap. I'm exhausted from earlier."

He nodded and almost walked out of the room, but he just couldn't do it. Not yet. He walked to the opposite side of the bed and leaned down to whisper in her ear. "I'll be back as fast as I can. Rest, please."

She nodded. Jensen straightened and headed out of the room to the elevator. As he was still waiting, Jakob came jogging down the hallway toward him.

"Mom wanted me to give you this, big brother," he said, handing Jensen the small ring case he recognized. "She thought it would be better at the house than around here. And truthfully, she's been a little out of it since we got the call. She was really upset."

"I know. Still bloody furious about Alfie myself. Not sure I'll ever get over it."

Jakob smiled. "Nicola is safe now, that's all that matters. Just make sure she says yes, because Mother might disown you and adopt Nicola if you don't."

He nodded. "I'll try my best. Get back in there and make sure Mother doesn't make a mess of it."

"Will do," he said, walking back to the room.

The door to the lift opened. Jensen stepped onto it and pushed the button to the ground floor. He just had to wait a day or two and he could set everything in motion. He also needed to make sure his mother didn't blow his proposal.

chapter nineteen

S he had been home from the hospital for less than two hours when Jensen came into her room with a smile on his face.

"What are you up to now?"

His smile dimmed a little. "What the bloody hell does that mean?"

"Well, you spring your brother and your mother on me. Thank goodness they had something to do today. Do you know how many times I have heard them tell me what a great catch you are?"

"Well, I am a great catch."

"No, you are not."

He opened his mouth to argue with her, but the doorbell rang. Then she heard voices—one robust and the other faint but unmistakable.

She felt tears burn the backs of her eyes.

"You brought my parents over?"

"Of course I did. They were adamant about coming, and I couldn't let them fly commercial," he said with such Wulf disdain she laughed, but it ended on a sob.

"I thought you would be happy."

She blinked and was, once again, horrified as tears slipped down her cheeks.

"I am. I'm sorry."

The noise grew as she listened to her parents coming up the stairs with Marta.

Jensen went to the door to greet them. "Mr. and Mrs. McCann. I trust your trip over was comfortable?"

"Sure was," her father boomed out. Nicola's father had always been loud, but he had started getting worse as the years went by. She didn't care. It was music to her ears. And he was the first one to step through the doorway.

"Nicola," her mother said as she followed him. Jensen stepped out of the way and her mother gasped.

"What happened to your face?" her father asked.

She glared at Jensen. "You told me it was getting better."

"It is." He looked at her parents. "It was much worse yesterday."

Her mother rushed to the side of her bed and her father to the other. "Oh, my baby, what did he do to you?"

"You should see the other guy," Jensen said, which earned him a glare from her mother. "Sorry, but she did beat Alfie up."

"That's because I taught her how to defend herself," her father said. He smiled, but she could see tears shimmering in his eyes. It almost broke her then and there. A lump rose in her throat. She'd never witnessed her father get choked up, let alone cry.

"I'm going to check with Marta about some coffee and snacks and leave you all alone," Jensen said.

"Jensen," she called out before he could run away. "Thank you for bringing my parents over."

"You are most welcome," he said before slipping out of the room and closing the door behind him.

"I was so surprised when he called us and said we just had to be here. We were already booking a flight, but it's hard to buy at the last minute," her mother said.

"And very expensive," her father commented.

Her mother waved that away as she sat on the bed next to Nicola. "Either way, we are here, but we got here a lot faster than if we had to fly commercial. And I'm sure much more comfortably."

"I'm just so happy that you're here."

Then, again, the tears started to flow as relief set in. No matter what had happened on the ice, Nicola had known her parents would always be there. She was over the age where she should need her parents; but having them there was a comfort. Jensen had known that. She knew he had come up with the idea on his own. Knowing him, he hadn't even told his mother or sister that her parents were there.

The fact that Jensen had been so sweet and thoughtful brought on a fresh wave of tears. They only had a couple more days here and she would be able to travel, and their time together would end. What the hell had she been thinking getting involved with him? Where would their relationship go afterwards? And why didn't she kill Alfie for taking away this precious time?

Her mother pulled her into a hug, being careful of her injured shoulder. The warmth of her arms, the familiar feeling of her mother's unconditional love filled her with twin emotions of joy and pain. She was losing something she didn't know she needed; but being here with her mother and father gave her some measure of comfort.

"Aw, baby, it's all right. We're here to take care of you."

And for that she would always be thankful. These two were always there for her.

"We would have been here faster but Denver International was closed down for twelve hours thanks to a freak blizzard," her father said.

She glanced at her side table. "I think it's time for another pill."

"Are you sure?" Her mother asked.

"Is Felicia here?"

"Who is that?"

"A nurse that Jensen hired."

Jensen opened the door. "Who did I hire?"

"Felicia? Is she here?"

"No. She's not here right now. She'll be back tonight. What do you need?"

It was then she noticed the fresh glass of water he was holding.

"I thought it was time for my pill."

"It is. Nadia, it's there on the table on your side. She needs just one."

He handed her father the water, then she took the pill from her mother. After she swallowed the medication, Jensen said, "Brett, I want to show you around a bit."

Her father nodded, then he leaned down to kiss her forehead. Jensen held the door open for him, and then gave her a warning look before he left the room.

"What was that look for?" her mother asked.

"That's his 'you better get rest' look. It's rather annoying."

Her mother chuckled. "You do need rest. A lot of it from what I gather. You were shot, Nicky."

Her mother hadn't used the nickname in years and it brought tears to Nicola's eyes. Once she'd hit her teenage years, she had insisted on Nicola or Nic, but the familiar endearment warmed her from the inside out.

"Oh, *Mama*. I'm so happy you are here."

"I am too. Your father was being stubborn and trying to insist that we take a regular flight, but everything was backed up for another two days. Jensen insisted that we come on the plane."

"He can be just as stubborn."

"Do you need me to leave you alone?"

"No, unless you want to."

"Of course not." She sat in the chair next to the bed. "Now tell me what is going on with Serenity."

Happy to have the focus off her and her injuries, Nicola smiled and told her mother of all the plans for the baby and Serenity's plans for a second book.

JENSEN WAS JUST POURING himself another cup of coffee when Nicola's father made his way downstairs. At first look, most people would look at Brett McCann and think that he looked nothing like Nicola. That all of her features came from her mother, but that wasn't true. Her incredible height was one thing, but also her nose. It wasn't small and delicate like her mother's. No, it was slender, and slightly turned up. When she spent a little too much time in the sun, she would get freckles just like her father had.

"I think it's time we had a talk, son."

He knew this was coming, and he had planned on making a stop on their trip back to England. That was before the shooting.

"Certainly. Do you want a cup of coffee?"

He shook his head. "I've already had too much of that evil brew. I need to sleep tonight."

"Let's go outside. Your daughter has amazing hearing and tends to eavesdrop."

"Got that from her mother," he said as he followed Jensen out the door. They continued walking until they were close to the beach. Neither of them had shoes on, so Jensen led him to the sand.

"Damn that feels good. Nadia and I have never been over here before."

"This house is open to both of you for whenever you want."

He glanced at Jensen. "I won't be bought off by pretty things."

Jensen laughed. "God, everyone thinks she's like her mother, but I think there is a fair amount of you in her."

Her father smiled at that, then it faded. Jensen knew the last seventy-two hours had been hard on them.

"I can't believe we almost lost her."

"I know and I'm sorry about that."

"You shot her?"

"No, but Alfie was my friend."

"You just never know. When I met Nadia, then married her, I lost a fair number of friends."

"What? Why?"

"She was from one of those *Soviet* countries, which meant she had to be a spy." Brett rolled his eyes. "Can you imagine? Like Nadia could ever hide anything from anyone. But what I'm getting at is that I thought all of those friends would accept her with open arms. Some of them I had known my whole life. So, you can't be blamed for that asshole's actions."

"Yes, sir."

"Now, I have a feeling you wanted to talk to me about something."

"Yes. I would like to marry Nicola."

"I had a feeling. What did she say?"

"I didn't ask yet. I was waiting for you to get here."

Brett's eyebrows shot up. "Oh, Nicola isn't going to like that."

"I don't care," he bit out. "Sorry. A friend said the same thing. There were other circumstances."

"What? What are you waiting for?"

"I wanted to make sure she wasn't feeling vulnerable." Then he stared at her father. "Wait, how did you know about all of this? How did you know I wanted to marry her?"

"It was in your voice on the phone. You sounded as if you were losing your entire world. I knew then you were in love with her. Because I would sound the same way if anything like this had happened to Nadia."

"I have your blessing?"

"Keep her safe and happy, then yes. I couldn't deny you, Jensen. You love her too much. Of course, I'm not the one you have to convince. And you better do it soon because I can't keep a secret from her mother. She'll figure it out and blab to Nicola."

"I have the ring and planned on it."

"Now, I think we need to clean up. Our bags aren't here though."

"I wanted to have you stay here, but my mother and brother came, and I have Felicia the nurse staying overnight. So, I booked you a suite at the Hilton."

"I can pay my own way."

This was just like the stupid argument over the plane. "I know you can, but you're going to be my father-in-law so get used to it."

Brett let out one of his booming laughs. "Yeah, I think you and Nicola will figure it out." He held out his hand. Jensen took it. "Welcome to the family, son."

NICOLA DOZED for a few hours and woke to silence. The room was dark, but she could see light from the hallway. Her eyes adjusted to the darkness as she looked around the room. It was then that she saw Jensen. He was sitting in the chair beside her bed. From his even breathing, she knew he was sleeping.

She watched him for a long time knowing that she wouldn't see him in this way for much longer. They only had a few days left in Hawaii and that would be the end of everything.

"Do you know how creepy it is to have you staring at me like that?" he asked.

She smiled. "What time is it?"

He opened his eyes and leaned forward to grab his phone off her bedside table. "Nine."

She frowned. "Where is everyone?"

"I sent them out. They were so loud I was afraid they would wake you, so your parents and my mother and brother went out to a Luau. I insisted they go and John drove them, so they could have all the Mai Tai's and Lava Flows they want."

She smiled. "Thank you."

He rose from the chair and sat down on the mattress next to her and took hold of her hand. "How are you feeling?"

"Good, I guess. Even though I've spent most of the last few days in bed, I'm still tired."

"The doctor said you needed time to heal."

Then, neither of them said anything. The silence stretched out to awkwardness.

"Well, I guess I need to start making arrangements for us to head back to England."

"I told Mother we're staying an extra week. The doctor doesn't want you to travel too soon."

"Ah."

"There was something I wanted to talk to you about. Well, a couple of things."

His serious tone worried her.

"Okay."

He turned on the bedside table lamp. She blinked at the sudden brightness in the room. When her eyes finally focused, she saw things she hadn't seen before. Jensen had dark smudges beneath his eyes, telling her he hadn't caught up on his sleep. In fact, he looked a little haggard thanks to the two day's growth of beard on his face. Why did that man look yummy even when he looked like a mess?

"First, when were you planning on telling me that Micah was your first Dom?"

Shock came first, then irritation. If Micah told him, she would smack him. "How did you find that out?"

"Serenity told me. Not on purpose, she just thought I knew and *you* are evading the question."

She slipped her hand from his and struggled trying to sit up, but it was difficult with her shoulder injury. Jensen helped her up and made sure she had enough pillows to support her.

"I don't know if I would have ever told you."

He frowned. "Why not? Don't you think I have a right to know?"

She shook her head. "I didn't think it was any of your business."

"Not any of my business," he blustered. "What the bloody hell does that mean?"

She sighed. "I don't know your first sub, now do I?"

"No, but—"

"So why do you think you have a right to know about my first Dom?"

"Because it's different."

"That makes no sense."

"What makes no sense is this stupid arrangement."

"Oh?" Her heart sank to her stomach. She had thought they could at least keep the relationship going for the duration of their time in Hawaii. There wouldn't be a lot of play thanks to her injury, but they could at least have some time together.

"We can't go on like this. It's too much to ask."

She nodded and prayed she would be able to hold back the tears. She wasn't one for crying, although she seemed to be doing a lot of that since her altercation with Alfie.

"Of course," Nicola agreed as she smoothed out her bedsheet. She kept her eyes averted so he didn't see her disappointment. Why did he have to turn the light on? This would have been better in the dark.

"That's why I think we need a change."

"What kind of change?"

"Are you going to just keep staring at the sheet or actually have the nerve to look at me?"

She drew in a deep breath and hoped the tears she felt in her eyes weren't easy to see. The humiliation would be too much. She raised her head and made eye contact. His gaze softened.

"Why do you look so sad?"

"It's the pain medication."

His mouth curved. "Is that a fact?"

"Don't you dare mock me," she said, trying to sound stern, but her sentence ended on a sob.

"Oh, love, don't cry. Please." When the comment just made her cry more, his voice turned panic. "I don't like it one bit. Stop it."

"I don't care," she said, the tears flowing down her cheeks. "If you're going to break it off, then I'm going to cry. Just deal with it."

He shook his head. "That isn't what I'm doing."

"Then what would you call it?"

"I would call it a bloody proposal, but you have ruined it by trying to control everything. I swear to God you don't take direction well unless there's a promise of a spanking."

"Well…wait, what?"

"I'm trying to propose."

"Like in marriage?"

"Yes, like in marriage."

"You don't want to get married."

He nodded. "I do. To you."

"No."

He blinked. "What?"

"I said no." She would not take his pity. That would be worse than indifference.

"Why not?" he asked, his voice in a near shout.

"Because you are doing this because you feel sorry for me."

He studied her for a long moment. "That's the biggest load of rubbish I've ever heard, and that's saying a lot."

"It isn't. You never wanted to marry."

"I did, once upon a time. I didn't have anyone in mind,

but I always wanted to marry, before I fell down the hole with a needle in my arm."

"Why did that change your mind?"

"I didn't think any woman would take a chance on me. I could hardly blame her. I'm a drug addict who has already had one relapse."

"*Three* years ago."

"And you were the one who pulled me out of that."

She shook her head. "I helped, but you did it yourself."

"See, it's that faith you had in me. You never doubted me."

"I gave you a choice. I did offer to kill you."

He chuckled. "That's true."

"But the real work was by you."

"This isn't an act? You really don't know, do you?"

"What?"

He took her hand again. "Nicola, you are the center of my universe. I can't think of losing you to anyone whether it's that bastard Alfie or two gay wankers who want to have a baby."

"Yeah?"

"Yes. That's why I made sure Mother had this with her." He dropped his hand, then pulled something out of his pocket. It was a small jewelry box. "It's not new. It was left to me by my grandmother."

He opened the box and turned it so she could see it. Set against the ruby background sat one of the most beautiful rings she had ever seen. The diamond was round cut, but smaller diamonds created a square frame. The band split slightly, each side of it also had diamonds.

"I know platinum isn't the first choice these days."

"It's beautiful," she said. She lifted her gaze to his. "I love it."

"So, will you wear it? Be my wife?" he asked, sincerity ringing in his tone, but she still needed to know.

"Why do you want to marry me?"

Nicola held her breath. He didn't lose his temper this time.

"Because I can't think of another woman I want in my bed or at my mercy more than you. Because these last four years have taught me that I need you in my life to feel complete." She opened her mouth, but he stopped her with his next sentence. "I love you, Nicola McCann."

"Oh," she said, tears welling up in her eyes once again. "I love you, too."

"Is that a yes?"

She nodded. "Yes."

He took her hand and slipped the ring on. "A little loose but we can fix that."

He leaned forward and brushed his mouth against hers. "Thank you."

"For saying yes?"

"For saving me four years ago and for not walking away a year later when I lost it again. And, for always accepting me for who I am. With your history, I'm amazed you even wanted to get involved with me."

"It's different. You always wanted to be better. Oliver didn't. It's easy to believe in someone when they tell you they want to recover."

He raised her hand to his lips. "You will always be the one person in the world I need by my side, in my business, and in my bed."

"Thank you."

"I really want to celebrate, but you can't right now."

She crooked her finger. "We can at least do a little necking,"

He smiled as he rose off the bed and then slipped beneath the sheets with her.

"One thing Wulf men do know how to do is please the women they love."

She slipped her one good arm over his shoulder. "I can attest that you are very good at that."

"Yes, but I think I have to prove myself after my botched proposal."

"I think it was beautiful."

Jensen was smiling when he bent his head as her heart filled with joy. She had the only Dom she could ever want all to herself. A woman couldn't ask for anything more.

epilogue

Nicola studied her reflection. The dress she had chosen for her wedding was deceptively simple. It hugged her slight curves and only showed a hint of her cleavage. Of course, she thought, turning around, the back was dramatic. It was ivory with blue hibiscus flowers on it. The ruffled neckline was similar to the Hawaiian dresses she loved. Everything about it made her feel sexy and beautiful—just like Jensen did.

"My brother is going to lose his cool when he sees that," Jules said, her voice filled with a mix of amusement and deep affection as she stepped up beside Nicola.

She shared a smile with Jules. "Yeah, well, it's good to remind Jensen that he doesn't always have to be in control."

Jules sighed, her smile dimming.

Nicola turned to face her friend. "What's going on?"

"Nothing." The fake smile did not sit well with Nicola.

"Jules, tell me."

"It's just the bastard I dumped. And yes, I am using that word because he deserves it."

"He's causing you more problems."

She wandered away to look out the window of their luxurious beachfront villa. They were in Hawaii for their wedding, surrounded by the serene beauty of the ocean. It was a private affair, with mainly close friends and family. Jensen grumbled about Micah being there, but she had ignored him. She knew that Jensen counted Micah as a friend and he was being a jealous prig.

"I wish I could just find a nice guy. Someone who likes me for me," she said, sadness pulling her tone down.

Nicola went to her then, wrapping her arm around her friend. "You will. I believe it," she said with unwavering conviction.

Jules dabbed away tears. "I don't know. Everyone knows who I am, and they assume they know me. That I'm a nympho of some sort." Her voice trembled with the weight of her words.

"Please let me make him cry."

A laugh bubbled up out of the younger woman. "I keep telling you no for a reason. You and Jen have been through enough."

Nicola sighed. She wanted to fix things for Jules but knew her soon-to-be sister-in-law needed time. She couldn't stand to see her hurting.

Jules rested her head on Nicola's shoulder.

"In less than an hour, you're going to be my sister-in-law for real," Nicola said, her voice filled with warmth and anticipation.

"Yeah." It was easy to hear the smile in her friend's voice. She lifted her head and wiped away her tears.

"Please let me make him cry."

A laugh bubbled up out of the younger woman. "I keep telling you no for a reason. You and Jen have been through enough."

Nicola sighed. She wanted to fix things for Jules but knew her soon-to-be sister-in-law needed time. She just couldn't stand to see her hurting.

Jules rested her head on Nicola's shoulder.

"In less than an hour, you're going to be my sister for real," Nicola said.

"Yeah." It was easy to hear the smile in her friend's voice. She lifted her head and wiped away her tears. "And I refuse to let that wanker ruin your day. And my day. It's not been fun dealing with two brothers. Now I'll have a sister by my side."

Nicola felt her own eyes burning.

"Oh, shit! I'm sorry," Jules said. "I didn't mean to upset you."

She shook her head and grabbed a tissue. She wasn't wearing that much makeup but didn't want to smear what she had on.

"I'm not upset. I'm happy. I always wanted a sibling. Being an only child was lonely."

"Hmm, I would say you were lucky. Imagine dealing with my two brothers your whole childhood."

The love she heard in Jules' voice made her smile. "Speaking of sexy, you in that dress…"

She laughed. "Thank you for letting me pick."

In another Hawaiian-themed dress, Jules had that same ruffled neckline but the shade of blue the flowers on Nicola's dress. "And as much as I love my shoes, I love being barefoot."

"Right?"

"What are you girls doing in here?" Her mother said, rushing into the room, her father strolling behind her. In that instant, she knew she would finally have what her parents had. That connection…that unconditional love. She and

Jensen will live the rest of their lives together, sharing in memories…good and bad…but they will weather any storm together.

"We were gossiping about how handsome Dad is," she said with a smile. Her parents wore matching outfits, the same shades that matched her flowers. They wore leis, her father's made of leaves, and her mother's matched their flowers. They were so cute together.

"I better get going before the idiot groom shows up complaining we're taking too long," Jules said. "See ya at the altar, sista." She added a lilt to her voice. She grabbed her simple nosegay of multicolored plumeria. It matched Nicola's, except that as the bride, she added a little cascade to the design.

"You look beautiful," her father said, a quiver of emotion in his tone.

She smiled, fighting tears. "Don't make me cry. My makeup is perfect."

"You're perfect. Always have been," he said, smiling at her. He had said that to her when she was growing up.

"Thank you. Now, Jules wasn't wrong. Jensen could show up being grumpy, so let's get going." She slipped her arm through each of theirs. "Thank you for being the best parents."

They walked to the door of the guest room. She drew in a deep breath and let the happiness bounce through her. They stepped out, and Jules and Serenity stood. Her friend had been indisposed…in other words, throwing up. The trio were expecting their first baby, and she couldn't be happier for them.

Her dress was of the same material as Jules, but Serenity's was tailored for her shorter, slimmer body. Tears filled her eyes.

"Oh, wow. I'm sorry I couldn't help you get dressed."

Nicola rolled her eyes. "Yeah, zipping up a dress was soooo hard."

She let go of her parents to hug her friend. "Don't worry, Mama," she whispered in her ear. When she drew back, both of them had tears in their eyes.

"Hey, ladies...and Mr. McCann?" Jackob called out. "Jensen is five seconds away from losing it."

She shook her head. "I guess that means he's getting grumpy. Let's get this show on the road."

* * *

Jules watched as her brother led Nicola out to the makeshift dance floor. His hand was on the small of her back.

She had been right. Her brother's reaction to the back of the dress had been hilarious and also cute at the same time. He pulled her into his arms, and the music started.

She glanced around at the crowd and realized this was the antithesis of any wedding she had been to. The weddings she attended were about impressing people with the price of the ceremony and reception. Nicola and Jensen were dancing around the floor, with a string of lights criss-crossing the dance floor...and it was perfect. No amount of money would have made it better than the love they shared.

She sighed, knowing that she envied their connection and that it would be nearly impossible to find because of who she was.

"What's up," Jakob said. She glanced at her brother, sporting a beard for his latest role. Her mother had been irritated, but Jules liked it.

"Nothing. Just a little jealous of their happiness. They're perfect for each other."

"Took him long enough."

She smiled as Jensen dipped Nicola, making her laugh.

"Yeah, but sometimes it takes a jolt to figure out who or what you want from life."

"And you realized that about the prick and we are all happier for it."

There was something in his tone that had her turning toward her brother. He was the proverbial middle child, probably feeling left out at times smashed between the oldest brother and the only girl. So, he had turned to acting. He still had a seat on the board, but everyone knew Jackob would become an actor even before he reached his teens.

And usually, he was better at hiding his feelings, but lately...he'd been off.

"What's up with you?"

"Nothing."

She frowned. "Jake...come on. It's me. Tell me."

Even with their age difference...not to mention their personalities, all the Wulf siblings were close.

"I screwed something up."

"So fix it."

"It's not that simple."

She laughed. "Which means you can't throw money at it."

"Bugger off," Jakob said as he drained the rest of his drink.

"Hey, I know I don't know much about the situation, and I have no real basis to give love advice."

His eyebrows shot up. "What makes you think it's about a woman?"

"You said you screwed something up, and you can't throw money at it."

He looked away and drew in a deep breath. "So? Your advice?"

She glanced out at Jensen and Nicola. "They waited years, but look how happy they are. I'm sure they screwed it up along the way, but they came out the other side together. Not without risks, Jake. If she's worth your love, you should be willing to chance everything to get her back."

"I never really had her," he murmured.

"Then do something about it because I learned in the last few months that settling won't make you happy."

He nodded and turned to leave. Then he turned back to her and kissed her cheek.

"Thanks, Jules."

Then, he wandered away just as the song was coming to an end. The smiles on the couple's faces warmed her heart. She wanted that. Jules wasn't sure she would ever be able to get it, but one thing she wasn't going to do anymore was settle.

Thank you so much for reading Faith! I hope you enjoyed Jensen and Nicola's story. If you did, please think about leaving a rating or review at your favorite online bookstore or review site!

Don't miss the next exciting book in The Wulf Family series! One-Click Taboo—->Preorder NOW.

Julienne Wulf has always played the good girl, but she's found a man who encourages her to be bad.
Check out an excerpt!

taboo is next!

"We might have a problem."

Julienne stared at him as if he lost his mind. "What do you mean?"

"We didn't use any kind of protection last night."

She blinked. "I'm on the pill, and I just had a check up."

He nodded. "I did too."

"So no worries there." She closed eyes and shook her head. "I don't know what has gotten into me."

"Me."

Her eyes shot open. "Alek, don't talk like that. Not here while we're at work."

"Now you're trying to play the good girl?"

"What do you mean by that? I have a reputation for being the one good sibling out of our family. Well, now Jensen is sober and has been for years, but I never did the kinds of things my brothers did."

He leaned closer and drew in a breath, his chest expanding and brushing against her breasts. With it came the scent of her, rose water and her own unique scent. Fuck, innocence and sin in rolled up in one woman. That contrast was so damned irresistible to him.

"I'm not talking about antics that land in you on the front page of the tabloids. I'm talking the two nights we shared. You remember those don't you?" She shivered. That was enough to tell him she did remember. He glanced down and saw her nipples hard against the silk fabric of her blouse. "You might play the good girl during the day, but at night you are definitely a very, very bad girl."

"Alek, they could return any minute and we're supposed to be professional."

He ignored her comments. Not because he didn't respect her, but he heard the arousal shimmering in her voice. It spoke to him on a level that he truly didn't understand.

"You can pretend to be that good girl, but I know the truth. When I have you beneath me and screaming my name, I'll be able to prove my point."

She turned to face him, and he saw it then. The shimmering heat in her eyes, but something else, something that tugged at his heart. She was ashamed of that. Ashamed of what made her feel good, and that was something he had to help her with.

"I am not a girl. I'm a woman."

She said it in the upperclass English prissy tone of hers that made him hot. With most women, it would be a turn off. With her...fuck, he wanted to strip her down and eat her delicious pussy. He was a sick, sick man.

"Oh, darlin'," he said, allowing his gaze to drift down to her breasts and back up again. "I know you are *all* woman."

Make sure to pick up Julienne and Alek's book, TABOO!

check out the new tfh team!

An exciting new romantic suspense series set in *USA Today Bestselling Author Melissa Schroeder's Harmless World!*

Each member of TEAM Bravo will be pushed to the brink as they start their duty as the main search and rescue division of Task Force Hawaii.

TEAM MEMBERS

- Captain: Seth Harrington
- Ryan Morrison w/ rescue dog Maya
- Nikki Kekoa
- Robbie Ramirez
- Kapone Hanson (Kap)

Check out BOOK ONE: *Justified Secrets*

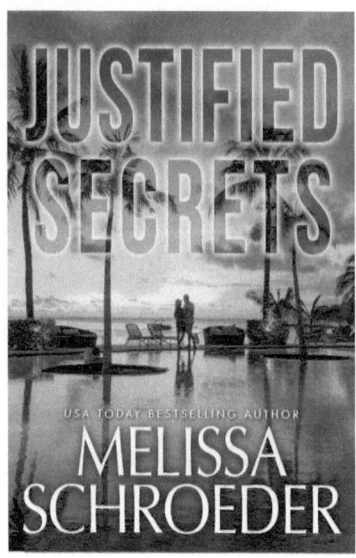

Everyone has secrets, but hers could get them both killed.

Autumn Bradford has always been a little…different. The daughter of a cult leader, she has spent her life fighting the bad guys and searching for the father everyone thinks is dead. One thing stands in her way, the new leader of Team Bravo.

Former SEAL Seth Harrington accepted the job at TFH for a new start. Years of dangerous missions has left his body and soul scarred. He doesn't have time for a woman with too many secrets and the eating habits of a hobbit-no matter how attractive he finds her.

Autumn doesn't need a keeper or a protector, but every time she turns around, Seth seems to be there. Time together makes it difficult to avoid their attraction, and one stolen kiss makes it impossible to resist the temptation. Falling in love wasn't in the plans for either of them, but Seth realizes he will do anything to protect her, even if it means facing down the most dangerous man either of them know: her father.

Author Note: This is a Harmless World Novel with our favorite crime fighting heroes and heroines! There are secrets (duh!), inappropriate jokes, Hawaiian food, a betting pool as usual, and a new team to get to know.

acknowledgments

As many readers know, this book was put on hold due to a personal health issue. I cannot say how much everyone's comments, thoughts, prayers, emails, and cards have meant to me.

A big shout out to the Addicts, who have been supportive since they were first founded on Facebook over seven years ago. Your support means more than you will ever know.

A big thanks to Noel Varner who worked with me over these last 7-8 months to get A Little Harmless Faith up to snuff, even with a broken finger. You are always so supportive of my work.

I am blessed with some amazing friends, including Joy Harris and Brandy Walker. Joy, you kept the Addicts hopping and made sure that everything ran smoothly. From the first moment of my diagnosis, Brandy, you have been there. From the care packages to the hat you made for me to your attendance at the Schroeder girls' sushi celebration, you have been the best friend any girl could want.

A big wet kiss to Les and my girls. They had a lot on their plates trying to take care of the family caretaker. Every appointment, every chemo infusion, Les, you were by my side. I don't know if I would have been able to handle it without you.

And last, but not least, to the entire staff at the Fair Oaks

Inova infusion center, but especially to Nurse Allison who saved my life more than once thanks to my allergic reactions. All of you are truly angels of the first order and I can never thank you enough.